love,
annie

Other books in the growing Faithgirlz!™ library

The Faithgirlz! ™ *Bible*
Faithgirlz! ™ *Backpack Bible*
My Faithgirlz! ™ *Journal*

The Blog On Series
Grace Notes (Book One)
Just Jazz (Book Three)
Storm Rising (Book Four)

Nonfiction
No Boys Allowed: Devotions for Girls
Girlz Rock: Devotions for You
Chick Chat: More Devotions for Girls
Shine On, Girl!: Devotions to Keep You Sparkling

The Sophie Series
Sophie's World (Book One)
Sophie's Secret (Book Two)
Sophie and the Scoundrels (Book Three)
Sophie's Irish Showdown (Book Four)
Sophie's First Dance? (Book Five)
Sophie's Stormy Summer (Book Six)
Sophie Breaks the Code (Book Seven)
Sophie Tracks a Thief (Book Eight)
Sophie Flakes Out (Book Nine)
Sophie Loves Jimmy (Book Ten)
Sophie Loses the Lead (Book Eleven)
Sophie's Encore (Book Twelve)

Check out www.faithgirlz.com

faiThGirLz!

love, annie

DANDI DALEY MACKALL

zonderkidz

ZONDERVAN.COM/
AUTHORTRACKER

zonder**kidz**.
The children's group of Zondervan

www.zonderkidz.com
Love, Annie
Copyright © 2006 by Dandi Daley Mackall
Illustrations © 2006 by The Zondervan Corporation

This is a work of fiction. The characters, incidents, and dialogue are products of author's imagination and are not to be construed as real. Any resemblance to actual events or persons, living or dead, is entirely coincidental.

Requests for information should be addressed to:
Zonderkidz
Grand Rapids, Michigan 49530

Library of Congress Cataloging-in-Publication Data

Mackall, Dandi Daley.
Love, Annie / by Dandi Daley Mackall.
       p. cm. -- (Faithgirlz)
    Summary: Annie, who maintains a blog advice column under the name "Professor Love," considers herself an expert on the subject of relationships until she gets her dream homecoming date and realizes how much she has to learn about both love and friendship.
    ISBN-13: 978-0-310-71094-3 (softcover)
    ISBN-10: 0-310-71094-4 (softcover)
       [1. Interpersonal relations–Fiction. 2. Dating (Social customs)–Fiction. 3. Self-perception–Fiction.
4. Christian life–Fiction.] I. Title. II. Series.
    PZ7.M1905 La 2006
    [Fic]–dc22
                                                                                          2005032136

Zonderkidz is a trademark of Zondervan.
Art direction: Laura Maitner-Mason
Illustrator: Julie Speer
Cover design: Karen Phillips
Interior design: Pamela J.L. Eicher
Interior composition: Ruth Bandstra

Illustrations used in this book were created in Adobe Illustrator.
The body text for this book is set in Cochin Medium.

Printed in the United States of America

07 08 09 10 • 10 9 8 7 6 5 4 3 2

So we fix our eyes not on what is seen, but on what is unseen.
For what is seen is temporary, but what is unseen is eternal.

— *2 Corinthians 4:18*

1

Annie Lind read the latest question emailed to the *That's What You Think!* website. It was a love question, and Annie's job was to field all questions about love. No problem. Not for "Professor Love," as Annie had started calling herself.

Grace Doe, a sophomore like Annie, had rounded up staff for her blog, which she called *That's What You Think!* Grace did most of the writing, putting out live journals about things she observed at Big Lake High School. But she'd recruited Annie to answer all love email.

"So?" Grace's long fingers drummed the back of the chair as she read the screen over Annie's shoulder. "Don't just sit there. How are you going to answer it, Annie?"

"I'm thinking!" Annie snapped. Grace could be so bossy. She and Annie had never been friends at high school. They had nothing in common. Annie belonged to everything — cheerleading, committees, Student Council. Grace belonged to nothing. Annie hated being alone. She needed her group of girls around her — or better yet, a group of guys. Grace, of course, liked to be alone. When Annie thought about it, it was pretty amazing that she and Grace could work together on anything.

Grace was growing on her, though. The girl saw things nobody else did. She knew when a teacher was going to explode, just by the way the teacher's nose twitched. She could tell if a guy was lying by what he did with his hands. She could see through people. Annie admired that.

She smiled up at Grace to make up for snapping at her. "Just give me a sec, okay?"

Annie scrolled down to see the other questions from readers. She winked at Mick, Grace's little stepsis, who was sprawled on the gigantic leather couch. The three of them had come straight to "the Cottage" after school so Annie could use the main computer and Mick could upload it to the blog site.

Annie wished she lived in a cottage like this. She loved everything about it — the big wooden beams, the fireplace, the white stucco walls. The plush, all-white furniture wouldn't have lasted thirty seconds at Annie's house, with Marbles the Mutt. Grace was so lucky. The cottage sat empty most of the time because Grace's real mom was usually off in Paris or London or someplace exotic. But she kept the cottage in their little town of Big Lake, Ohio, so Grace could use it whenever she felt like it. Since Grace had recruited her "blog team," they'd started using the cottage as a base camp.

The team consisted of Grace and Mick; Jazz, the artist; Storm, the trivia queen; and Annie. Each of them had a section of the website, and the whole thing was anonymous. Jazz did graphics and came up with cartoons that rocked. Storm wrote the same way she talked, spilling out all kinds of funny facts about everything. Annie, as "Professor Love," was supposed to do an advice column. She liked being

Professor Love, but she was so busy she couldn't waste much time with it today.

She finished reading the last question and got ready to answer. "No sweat, Grace. Prof Love is on the case!"

• •
THAT'S WHAT YOU THINK!
by Jane
SEPTEMBER 8

> *Dear Professor Love,*
>
> *I am SO in love with this boy @ my school, but i can't get him 2 love me back. I've done everything. I know his work and practice schedules, so I go 2 all his football practices and shop @ his store until I'm flat broke. I know his class schedule, and I dress hot every day and wait 4 him outside his classroom. Sometimes i drive by his house, just so i can "feel" his presence and hope he'll feel mine. What else can I do 2 make him love me?*
>
> *— Desperate*

> *Dear Desperate,*
>
> *So what is your plan here? Stalk him and hope he'll panic and give in? There are laws against you, you know. Did you ever hear of a time-tested strategy called "playing hard to get"? No? Didn't think so. Try it! Soon — before the police show up on your doorstep. There's a chance — a small chance — that he'll miss your*

adoration and wonder why you no longer know he exists.
True, he may just be glad to be rid of you. But even so,
isn't it better to move on than to be locked up in juvie for
stalking?

—Love, Professor Love

Dear Professor Love,

My boyfriend is picky. My girlfriends say he's controlling.
I'll show up for our date in a skirt, and he'll suggest I go
back and change into jeans. Another night, I show up
in jeans, and he asks why don't I wear that red dress he
likes. I guess it's more than clothes. He's always telling me
not to laugh so loud, or to wear my hair up, or he's telling
me to learn more about art and music. I don't want to
make him mad or anything. But do you have something I
could tell him?

—Unsure

Dear Unsure,

Yeah. Tell the loser that you're not Burger King, and he
can't have it his way.

—Love, Professor Love

Dear Professor Love,

All year I've been trying to ask out this hot girl in my English class. She's all I can think about — perfect bod, perfect everything. Only thing is, I've noticed that she can be, well, mean to other people. We sit next to each other in class, and she's always bagging on this heavy girl who sits in front of us. And she giggles when a kid in our class, a special-needs guy, answers a question wrong. Plus, she's always gossiping about other girls we know.

So, any advice for me?

— Starstruck

Dear Starstruck,

Here's my advice: See no evil. Hear no evil. Date no evil.

— Love, Professor Love

"Sweet!" Grace exclaimed as soon as Annie quit typing. "I couldn't have come up with those answers in a million years."

Annie leaned back in the cushy desk chair and sighed. "Nothing to it, when you're Professor Love. I think I was born to be a professor of love."

Mick came over and read the screen. "Annie, have you always known what to say to boys?"

Annie thought about it. "Well, since the age of four, anyway."

"Great," Mick muttered. "Want me to upload it now?"

Michaela, or "Mick," was only in seventh grade, three years behind Annie and Grace, but she was the computer genius who'd set up the blog and kept it going. She helped out at Sam's Sammich Shop, Annie's mom's place, all the time. Mick was like the little sister Annie never had. One night each week, Mick had dinner at Annie's house, and Annie knew her mom looked forward to it as much as Annie did. Girlfriends her own age had come and gone for Annie. Boyfriends too. But Mick had always been there.

"All yours," Annie said, giving up the computer chair.

As usual, Mick's long, brown ponytail was pulled back through the hole in her Cleveland Indians ball cap. One of these days, Annie planned to take Mick under her wing and teach her to dress like a girl. She was already fiercely cute. In a couple of years, Mick would be amazing, inside and out.

Mick took over at the keyboard and started her magic. "I was hoping to talk to you about something, Annie."

"Sure, Munch." Annie could never say no to "Mick the Munch."

"Great! I'll be done with this in just a minute." Mick popped in her keychain drive and hit Save.

Somebody's cell went off. Annie and Grace grabbed for their bags. It was Grace's. She flipped up her cell lid. "Hello? Hey, Storm. Where are you? You owe me a trivia column."

There was a pause. Storm Novelo had moved to Big Lake the last week of August, just after school started. She was a freshman and two years younger than Annie and Grace. But Annie liked hanging out with her. She was so kickin' cool. Nobody dressed like Storm Novelo.

"Yeah," Grace was saying into the cell, "well, I've got to have it by Saturday."

Grace listened, her ear pressed to the cell. Her gaze shot to Annie. "She's here. Just a minute." Grace passed her cell to Annie. "Storm wants to talk to you."

Annie took the phone. "Hey, girl!"

"Hey yourself," Storm answered. "Thought you might be with Gracie. You better charge your cell. I couldn't get it to ring. Guess where I am?"

"Ummm ... the mall?"

"Nope."

"School?"

"Guess again."

"Home?"

Grace broke in with her deep, loud voice. "Excuse me! You're on my cell minutes. Play guessing games on your own time."

"I heard," Storm said, before Annie could repeat the warning. "I'm at a little place called Sam's Sammich Shop."

"I should have told you I wasn't working today," Annie said. She didn't work there every day because of cheerleading practices and other stuff. Today, her grandparents were covering for her. "Maybe I'll come by later if — "

"Later?" Storm interrupted. "Something tells me you're going to get your first speeding ticket getting over here right now. Or you would, if you actually had your license."

"Why?"

"Because guess who's here, sitting at a booth on the other side of the room."

"Ummm ..."

Grace glared at her. Annie wondered if she knew they were starting another guessing game.

"Just tell me!" Annie demanded.

"Sean."

"Get out! No way!" Annie cried.

"Way."

Annie chewed on a piece of her hair that had just gotten long enough to chew on. "When did he get there? Do you think he's looking for me?" Sean Davis was the hottest guy at Big Lake, and Annie was in love with him. Totally in love with him. Never mind that they hadn't actually gone out yet. She knew. She just knew. And she was sure he felt it, too. It was like they were soul mates.

"If he *is* looking for you," Storm commented, "he's not looking very hard. In fact, he's sitting across from Bridget, laughing at something she said."

"Get out! He is not!"

Bridget Crawford was the other sophomore cheerleader. Annie had heard that Bridget and Greg had broken up last weekend. The girl was on the prowl already.

"Just thought you'd want to know," Storm said.

"Yeah. Good lookin' out. Thanks, Storm. Can you tell if — "

"Oops. I've got another call."

"Don't let him leave, Storm! I'll be right there!"

Storm had already ended the call. Annie passed the cell back to Grace. "Thanks. I've gotta bounce."

Annie checked herself in the bathroom mirror before heading out. Her auburn hair looked good, straight and shiny. She'd have given anything, though, to have Grace's thick, blonde hair, which was straight without having to be straightened.

Mick and Grace were waiting for her when she came out of the bathroom. They all left together.

"You know," Grace said as she locked the door to the cottage, "I was thinking. Maybe you could write a special feature on the blog. Something on homecoming. Pretty universal, whacked-out craziness there. Great material, with all those couples on the verge of doing stupid things."

Annie laughed. "Ever the romantic, aren't you, Grace?" As far as Annie knew, Grace had never attended a homecoming dance or even a football game.

"Who are you going to homecoming with, Annie?" Mick asked.

Annie had almost forgotten Mick was there.

"Well," she began, "I guess it won't hurt to tell you guys." After all, it wasn't like Grace and Mick would broadcast it. Grace hardly talked to other kids at high school. And Mick was in middle school. "I'm going with Sean Davis. Just don't tell anybody."

Grace tucked the key into the pocket of her oversized black jeans and kept walking. "Okay. But why is it such a big secret?"

"Because," Annie admitted, "Sean doesn't know yet."

2

Annie raced down the walk, wishing she had her real driver's license. What good was a dumb learner's permit, when you had to take your mom with you everywhere?

"Bye, Annie!" Mick called.

Annie waved good-bye to Mick and Grace and dashed across King, so she could take the shortcut to the sandwich shop.

It was time for "Operation Sean" to kick up a notch. She and Sean had been flirting hard for days at school and after football practice, when Annie just happened to stop by the field. But she only had two weeks to get him to ask her to homecoming. She should have been dated up by now. Not that she hadn't had the chance. Annie had been asked by eight guys already. She'd managed to turn them all down, convincing each one that it broke her heart to say no.

But she'd decided the minute she'd broken up with Nate, or maybe it was Michael, that Sean was the one for her. With only two weeks left, even she had to admit that the timing was a challenge. But Annie Lind liked challenges.

At least her spies assured her that Sean hadn't asked anybody else yet. And Annie wasn't settling for anyone else either. She and Sean were going to homecoming together, whether he liked it or not. But of course, he'd like it.

A flock of geese honked overhead, and she glanced at the sky to see a slightly crooked V flying back north. It wasn't even officially fall yet, but the weather had already gone from chilly in early September back to hot. Annie wondered if the poor geese were mixed up and didn't know which way to go.

She burst into Sam's Sammich Shop, then tried to act as if she'd been strolling by. Beatles music played from the jukebox. Her mom, with Granny and Gramps Lind's help, had decorated the place '60s rock style. And for some reason, kids seemed to love it. Sam's Sammich Shop was the number one high school hangout. Black-and-white posters hung on one wall above the booths. On the back wall was a beach mural that could have fooled the Beach Boys.

"Hi, Annie!" her mom shouted from behind the counter. Samantha Lind had put every cent she had into the shop, and it had paid off. Sort of. They weren't rich by a long shot, but they made the mortgage payments on the shop and the house.

"Hey, Mom!" Annie spotted Granny Lind at the ice-cream machine. "Hi, Granny!"

Granny nodded and smiled, a cone in each hand. Annie's mom said she didn't know how she would have gotten along without her in-laws. Annie's dad had died in a plane crash when Annie was only two months old. But she felt as if she'd known John Lind. She knew what he was like when he was a kid. He'd had big feet and an even bigger heart. She knew he liked to play all sports, but he also liked to draw. She'd heard stories from her grandparents and more stories from her mom. As far as Annie knew, her mother had never even thought about dating. That's how much in love she'd been with Annie's father.

It was weird, the way Annie missed her dad, even though she'd barely had him in her life. All her memories of him were secondhand, but they were as real as if they'd been her own.

"Annie!" Storm Novelo strutted up in a short skirt that looked like a Scottish kilt, and a ruffled white blouse that made her look like she was ready for a duel.

Annie would have gladly traded her auburn head to have Storm's long, black hair. Storm was exotic and petite. She claimed to be mestizo, part Mayan and part Spanish, and Annie believed her. She was five feet two, eight whole inches shorter than Annie. And her shoe size, 5, was four and a half sizes smaller than Annie's monster feet, although Annie would never, ever let anybody at school know her shoe size.

The jukebox changed to "I Want to Hold Your Hand." Annie's sentiments exactly.

"Where is he?" she whispered. She didn't want to look for herself and appear to be searching for him, which she was.

Laughter burst from a back booth.

"Follow the laughter," Storm said. "Bridget's on a roll."

"I'd like to roll Bridget," Annie muttered. Bridget and all the cheerleaders knew Annie and Sean had been talking. She should have stayed away.

Annie risked a glance toward the booth. Bridget was picking a fry from Sean's plate, a begging look on her face. Right out of Annie's playbook!

"Come on!" She took Storm's elbow and dragged her toward the booth.

"Okay," Storm said. "But you might want a hair-check first."

Annie dropped Storm's elbow and felt her head. Her hair did feel messed up. "Why didn't you say something before?" She dashed to the bathroom, motioning for Storm to follow.

Even the restroom had the old-fashioned rock look. Gramps Lind had rigged it up so the music played through every room in the shop. Tiny black records with holes in the middle, "45's," Mom called them, hung on the walls.

Annie and Storm both worked on Annie's hair, trying to make it stay down and look straight instead of curly.

"So what's the plan, man?" Storm asked. "'Cause I love your mom and all, but I'm ready to fly out of here. Do you have any idea how many Coca-Colas will be consumed in the next hour? Twenty-seven million! True, not all of them here. But that's like, over six hundred million a day! Makes me nervous."

Storm Novelo knew this stuff off the top of her head. Annie thought she was probably a genius. But she understood why Storm didn't let on. Guys couldn't have handled it. It had been the right move on Storm's part to join Grace's blog team. The website was the perfect place for Storm to spill all her facts, anonymously.

Annie put on fresh lipstick, then turned to Storm. "All right. This is top secret, Storm. The plan is to get Sean to ask me to homecoming."

"Big flash," Storm said, her lips twisting into a smirk. "Like I didn't know that already?"

"Oh." Annie hoped she hadn't been that obvious to Sean. "You don't think he's already asked *her*, do you, Storm?"

"Man, I hope not!" Storm answered. "Then you'd only have — what — twenty guys to choose from? We'd have to call 911."

"Funny," Annie said, straightening the collar on her blue top, which exactly matched her eyes. "It doesn't matter how many ask, if the right one doesn't ask." *Annie's Rule.*

"Deep. Could I quote Professor Love on that?" Storm checked herself out in the mirror. Then she whipped out a silver barrette and brushed her hair up, catching it on one side. It took two seconds and looked elegant.

Annie knew that if she tried to do that with her hair, it would look ridiculous.

"Ready?" Storm asked.

Annie took a deep breath. "Ready! Operation Sean, Stage Two, is about to begin!"

They pushed out of the restroom as two younger girls came in.

"I won't even ask what Stage One was," Storm said. "What's Stage Two?"

"Stage Two is where Sean asks me out for this weekend, in preparation for asking me to homecoming."

"Taking it down to the wire, aren't you?" Storm asked as they passed the silver counter stools. "I heard Cody asked you to homecoming."

"Yeah." Annie had felt bad for Cody. They'd been pretty good friends when they were kids. They lived on the same street, went to the same church. They'd even gone on a few group dates together. Annie's mom was big on group dating. Annie wondered what her dad would have said on the subject.

At least Annie had let Cody down easy. He was a nice guy.
Cute too. He just wasn't Sean. "Did he get another date?"

Storm shrugged.

Annie didn't have time to worry about Cody now. He'd
bounce. Boys always did. Right now she needed to focus on
Sean. "Hi, guys!" Annie marched back to the booth and acted
surprised to see them all there.

On one side sat Sean and Stephen, a junior on the football
team. On the other side, Bridget and Merilee. Annie smiled
warmly at the boys.

Sean scooted over and patted the booth. "Here you go,
Annie. Have a seat."

Storm didn't get such a warm welcome from the girls' side.
She had to sit on the edge of the seat, then wriggle herself
over. "Thanks, girls!" she said, as if they'd both stood up to
make room. "Isn't this cozy?"

Annie picked a fry off the plate and ate it in teeny bites,
unlike Bridget, who scarfed hers down in one bite.

"Did you know," Storm began, "that man is the only animal
who will eat with an enemy?"

Annie muffled her laugh. Merilee and Bridget stared at
Storm as if she were a science experiment.

Stephen couldn't take his eyes off Storm, and Annie could
tell the boy liked what he saw. "So how do you like it here in
Big Lake, Stormy?" he asked.

"Storm," she corrected him firmly. "Well, Stevie, you don't
move here for the weather, do you? Or for the big lake?"

"There's really not a big lake in the whole town, you know,"
Stephen said.

"Nothing gets past you, huh, Stevie," Storm replied.

Annie tried not to laugh. Poor Stephen. If he was hitting on Storm, he had no idea what he was getting in for.

"So," Sean said, smiling down on Annie. He had the most beautiful white teeth Annie had ever seen. "Where've you been? I thought you'd be here after school."

Aha! Annie liked that. Sean had come here to see her. *Yes!*

"Here and there," she answered mysteriously. *Annie's Rule: Keep a guy guessing. It lets you live in his head.* "Had to help a friend with this computer thing."

"You're into computers?" Bridget asked. "I'm such an airhead when it comes to computers and stuff like that."

Bridget had aced computer class last year. Annie knew this because they'd been in the same class, the class Annie had gotten a B in. Obviously, Bridget still bought into the whole theory that guys prefer airheads. This, Annie knew, was unfortunately true in many cases. Probably not in Sean's case. She hoped he was deeper than that.

Still, better safe than sorry. "Me? Into computers?" Annie laughed. "My computer help comes in the form of moral support only. Seriously, technical things are just so ... so ..."

"So technical?" Storm offered.

Bridget salted what was left of the plate of fries. Some of the salt spilled onto the table. "Oops!" she squealed. She pinched the loose salt, then threw it over her shoulder. "Bad luck to spill salt," she explained.

"Not in Japan," Storm said. "It's good luck in Japan."

"Sweet!" Stephen exclaimed.

Bridget's friend Merilee frowned at Storm. "How do you know so much?" she asked.

Annie could tell Storm wished she hadn't said anything. She shrugged. "I saw it on TV," Storm answered. Annie knew for a fact that Storm's family didn't have cable TV. Besides, Annie was always catching Storm in the school library or the Big Lake Public Library. Storm read books, seriously heavy books.

They joked around until the fries were gone. Annie watched Bridget. Her brand of flirting was over the top. No doubt it worked on some guys, but the girl needed a softer sell.

"Let's talk football," Annie said, changing the subject from Bridget's boring story about her crummy Spanish teacher. Annie's Rule: Talk about things that interest guys — like sports and themselves. They'll think you're fascinating, and you won't have to say a word.

"Now you're talkin' my language," Sean said.

"So," Annie continued, making a point to stare into Sean's big brown eyes, "what's your strategy against the Wolverines?"

Sean talked on and on about running games and defense and third-down plays. Annie stared intently into his eyes the entire time. She watched his lips move. She could have listened — okay, so she wasn't exactly listening — to him forever.

"Well, I think you boys should seriously consider new outfits," Storm broke in. "I mean, excuse me, but which of you geniuses thought green and gold went together?"

"This from the queen of fashion?" Bridget asked, laughing, as if Storm too would think this clever.

Annie knew better. She braced herself.

Storm turned slowly to Bridget and looked her over, up and down. Bridget was prep all the way, with a plaid vest over her navy skirt and pink blouse. "You know, Bridget," Storm began, "I thought about becoming Barbie, like you. But I guess I'm just too lazy to keep up the bleach job on my hair." She moved closer to Bridget and squinted at her long blonde hair, which Annie knew for a fact was bleached. "How long did it take the roots to grow back to black like that?"

Bridget glanced at Sean, then back to Storm. Her face twitched into a dozen expressions, as if searching for the right one. "I — I don't bleach my hair!" She giggled nervously.

Now Storm did laugh with her. "Right."

After a minute of awkward silence, which Annie thoroughly enjoyed, Stephen brought them back to football. "I think the guys are really coming together," he said. "After practice yesterday, Coach Ramsey gave us the team spirit lecture, and I think it worked. We had this big group hug and — "

"Big, sweaty group hug?" Storm asked, scrunching up her face. She circled her arms over her head. "Over-sharing, Stevie."

Merilee cleared her throat. She usually didn't speak, except to echo Bridget. Merilee looked like a Bridget wannabe, but not quite. Her hair was blonde, but not thick and long like Bridget's. She dressed in the same preppy style, but her clothes were probably three sizes larger than Bridget's.

Annie wanted to draw her out. "Do you like football, Merilee?"

Merilee glanced at Bridget, as if to get an okay. But Bridget just frowned and looked bored.

Annie tried again. "I think you were going to say something about the team, right, Merilee?"

Merilee licked her lips, then blurted out, "I still can't believe Coach Ramsey is getting married."

Annie smiled at her. Annie had been invited to the wedding. Coach had invited all the players and cheerleaders. "I think it's great Coach is getting married. But what I can't believe is that his bride-to-be agreed to getting married on the football field. What is that about?"

"Hey!" Sean said. "I think that's cool. Coach practically lives on that field. She might as well get used to it."

A tiny alarm went off inside Annie, but she slapped it off. She knew Sean didn't mean it. They were all just kidding around.

"So you really think they'll go through with the wedding?" Storm asked.

"They got their license and everything," Sean answered. "Coach showed us."

Storm smirked. "Yeah? Well, every year about nine thousand couples take out marriage licenses and never use them. Anyway, when's the wedding supposed to be?" Storm kicked Annie under the table.

Annie knew that Storm knew the answer.

"Next Saturday. Same day as the homecoming dance," Sean said.

From your mouth to God's ears, Annie thought. It occurred to her that her mom would have thought that and meant it. Mom prayed about everything. So did Mick. Annie believed prayer worked too, most of the time anyway. It's just that she usually forgot to pray for things until it was too late.

"Earth to Annie?" Sean slurped the last of his chocolate milk shake and came up with a chocolate mustache on his upper lip.

Annie thought he looked adorable. She put one hand on his shoulder — the guy had definitely been working out. With her other hand, she used her napkin to dab off the mustache. *Annie's Rule: Seize every opportunity to show the guy he needs you, even in the little things of life.*

"There," she said, reluctantly moving her hand. "Are you guys coming by and hanging out here Friday night after the game?"

"Sure!" Stephen said, glancing over at Storm. "Will you guys be here?"

"*I* will be!" Bridget exclaimed, way too eager.

Annie sighed. "Depends."

"What do you mean?" Sean asked.

Annie shrugged slightly. *Ten, nine, eight ...* "Wow! It's getting late. I better go." *... seven, six, five ...* She scooted to the edge of the booth and stood up. "Coming, Storm?"

Four, three, two, ...

"Hey, Annie," Sean said. "Wanna meet me here after the game on Friday?"

Gotcha! "*This* Friday?" Annie asked.

"Yeah. After we crush the Wolverines," Sean explained.

Annie gave him her best smile. *You've earned it*, she thought. *So have I.*

3

Annie made her exit from the booth, conscious that Sean's gaze was undoubtedly on her.

Annie's Rule: Always assume you're being watched by Mr. Wonderful when you enter or exit the scene.

Storm caught up with her as she passed the counter. "A date with Sean. Professor Love strikes again. I'm impressed."

"Elementary, my dear Storm," Annie whispered, tossing her hair casually, the way women did in TV commercials.

"Annie!" Mick came jogging into the shop and straight up to Annie. "Good. You're still here."

"Not for long, Munch," Annie said, wanting to get away with a clean exit.

"But you said — ," Mick began.

"Annie," her mom interrupted, "your grandpa could use some help in the back." She tore off a bill from her pad and set it in front of one of the customers at the counter. The stools were full.

"I can't, Mom!" Annie protested. "We're starting homecoming decorations." Annie glanced at her watch. "Ten minutes ago. I'm late. Hamlet will rag on me all night if I don't leave right now." She risked a glance back at Bridget, who was still glued to Sean's booth. Apparently, Miss Homecoming Committee Chairwoman, aka Teacher's Pet, could get away with anything.

"Did you say 'Hamlet'?" Granny Lind asked. She set two glasses of ice water in front of two middle-school girls at the counter. They didn't even bother to say thank you.

"Mr. Hamilton, our English teacher," Annie explained. "I don't know who died and made him homecoming chaperone, but it was a big mistake."

Storm laughed.

"Why would you say a thing like that?" asked Annie's mom.

"Because it's the truth," Annie answered. "He's got about as much of a sense of humor as an amoeba. He's a dictator. Homecoming's supposed to be fun. But all he does is gripe at us."

"Well, maybe you're not giving him a fair chance, Annie," said her mother, fidgeting with the silver napkin holder.

Storm shook her head. "Man, if anybody's ever on my case — in front of me or behind my back — I hope you're around to defend me, Mrs. Lind."

"I remember a teacher I had who was just like that," Granny chimed in. "My old history teacher — what was his name? Cox? Wilcox? Anyway, that man knew how to take the fun out of everything."

"Now, Mom," Annie's mom began. "You don't know that *this* teacher is like that, just because — "

"Hey!" Gramps yelled from the back. "Could I get some help back here, please?"

Annie's mom turned to her. "Annie? We're so busy, and Megan's out sick."

"I know. I'm sorry. But I'm not kidding, Mom. Hamlet doesn't accept excuses. If we don't show, he'll probably cancel homecoming. I could close tonight. And open tomorrow if you want?"

"I'll help," Mick offered.

"Mick, could you?" Annie's mom seemed almost as relieved as Annie felt. She turned to Annie. "Don't be late for dinner, though. This is Mick's night to eat with us."

Annie kissed the top of Mick's head. "Munch, you are an angel! I owe you big!"

"Okay," Mick answered, moving behind the counter. "I'll collect when you and I have that talk, okay?"

Annie didn't get it. "Talk?"

"Yes, talk. Remember? I wanted to talk to you about ... about something?" Mick tugged her ponytail and raised her eyebrows.

Then Annie remembered. Mick had asked to talk to her back at the cottage. "Mick, I'm so sorry! I forgot! Tell me — fast." She glanced at her watch again. Fifteen minutes late.

"Help!" Grandpa Lind hollered from the back.

"No. That's okay," Mick said. "I need to help Mr. Lind. We can do it later."

"Annie!" Storm called. She was at the door, holding it open. "Are you coming or what?"

"I'm coming!" Annie hollered. She turned back to Mick. "We'll talk later, okay?"

Mick nodded. "Go!"

"Thanks, Mick!" Annie called back as she ran to catch up with Storm. "I'll make it up to you!"

Big Lake High was a two-story brick building that sat across the courtyard from the middle school. Annie and Storm hurried down the hall to the shop classroom, where they were supposed to meet with the homecoming committee.

"I'd like to take shop," Storm said as they slipped into the big, dusty room, where students learned to build shelves and tables and who-knew-what-else from wood. "Do you have any idea of the percentage of female architects versus male architects?"

"Nope," Annie replied. "Now, if they offered shop-*ping*, instead of shop, I'd sign up with you."

Wood shavings lay in the corners of the cement floor, and dust hung in the air. About a dozen students sat on the floor, wrestling with chicken wire and facial tissues. Annie hadn't thought much of the committee's plan to turn the gym into a garden of flowers, with tissue-stuffed arches. That stroke of un-genius had come from Chairwoman Bridget.

Annie and Storm slipped to the back of the room and plopped down next to Jazz. Jasmine Fletcher was thin, like a dancer, with thick, wavy, black hair. She was wearing jeans with layered shirts. But somehow, on Jazz, the outfit looked like high fashion. She was a real artist, which was why they'd all talked her into being on the homecoming committee. Jazz's idea had been to decorate with nothing but lighting. The way she'd described it, the gym would have rocked.

Jazz glanced up from the chicken wire strewn across her knees. "What is wrong with this picture?" she asked. "Is it just me, or does this have the feel of old-fashioned homecoming float written all over it?"

"You can blame our homecoming chairwoman for that one," Annie said. Bridget had pretty much appointed herself to the job when Hamlet asked who wanted to be chairwoman. Her hand had shot up first. Then, instead of holding a vote like a normal person, Hamlet had said, "Okay. Bridget is chairwoman, then."

"Speaking of our esteemed chairwoman," Jazz said, "where is she?"

"Last seen at Sam's Sammich Shop," Storm answered, "flirting with Annie's true love."

"Which would be ...?" Jazz began.

"Sean, of course!" Annie supplied.

"So Sean's the flavor of the week?" Jazz asked.

Annie elbowed her. "Not funny. This is the real deal, Jazz." Okay. Maybe not. But it felt real enough.

"Mmm-hmmm."

"You know, if you girls are going to show up late, the least you can do is work." Holden Hamilton, aka Hamlet, stood behind them, gazing down. His thick lock of sandy-blond hair flopped over one eye. He wore a navy turtleneck and blue jeans. Annie had to admit that if he weren't so old, he'd probably have been handsome.

"Good point, Mr. Hamilton," Storm said. She pulled a handful of tissues from the box on the floor and started stuffing them all into one hole.

Annie and Jazz laughed. Mr. Hamilton shook his head and strolled off.

"See?" Annie whispered. "No sense of humor."

"True," Storm said. "But he wins the Big Lake High Cutest Teacher Award. You have to admit."

"Gross," Annie said. She knew kids sometimes got crushes on teachers, but she'd never understood the phenomenon. Grace claimed there were signs that Bridget had a crush on Hamlet — the way Bridget's eyes widened whenever Hamlet walked into a room, her forced laughs and fidgets. And Grace Doe was almost never wrong about the signals she observed. Annie figured that if Hamlet even suspected Bridget had a crush on him, he'd move to Stratford-upon-Avon. Who could blame him?

"Well," Jazz commented, "the man gives me a headache."

"Unmarried women under the age of twenty-one are the most likely candidates for a headache," Storm said. "But get this. Almost nobody in mental hospitals ever gets a headache. Isn't that tight?"

Jazz rubbed her temples, then went back to tissue stuffing. She worked different-colored tissues into wires, making cool patterns. "Anyway," she began, "did Mick talk to you about tryouts, Annie?"

"Tryouts?" Annie asked. "We didn't get a chance to talk. What's the Munch trying out for?"

"Baseball. What else?"

"Why does she want to talk to me? I'm horrible at sports," Annie admitted.

"Mick's trying out for the middle-school team this year," Jazz explained. "Not enough girls went out to have a girls' team, so Mick wants to join the boys'. My little brother, Ty, made the team last year. He says Mick's a pro. He thinks she'll be the best pitcher in the league."

"Way to go, Mick!" Storm exclaimed. She wasn't even trying to stuff chicken wire. Instead, she was reading the fine print on the tissue box, a hairspray can, and a pack of gum.

"So what's the problem?" Annie asked.

"Mick hasn't said anything to me," Jazz explained, "but Ty says she's worried about the 'all-guy' part of playing for an all-boys' team."

"Hence the need for Professor Love," Storm deduced.

"Shh!" Annie wanted to keep her blog identity secret. Grace and Storm had almost convinced her that nobody else at Big Lake High would ever stumble onto the *That's What You Think!* website. But just in case, Annie planned to stay anonymous. That way, she was freer to shoot from the hip with her advice and not risk getting people mad at her.

"Speaking of Professor Love," Jazz whispered, "cool advice column."

"Is it up already?" Annie asked.

"Yup. Yours too, Storm. Great stuff."

"Did you do a cartoon for it?" Storm asked.

Jazz nodded.

"I want to see," Storm announced, getting to her feet. "Let's go check out a library computer. I know the online code." She brushed sawdust off her short skirt and tights. "Besides, this place is filled with nastiness."

"Sweet!" Annie bounced up too. She didn't even bother to ask Storm how she knew the code for the library computers. Storm simply knew stuff. "You coming, Jazz?"

"What, and miss using my artistic talents here on the floor with these tissues? Not on your life." Jazz waved them off. Annie saw that each of Jazz's fingernails had an original painted design.

Annie and Storm slipped out of shop while Hamlet was breaking up an argument on the far side of the room. They hurried down the hall and headed for the library. As they passed the main door, Annie glanced outside. A yellow Volkswagen sat idling by the curb.

"Hey, look! It's Sean!" Annie bolted for the door. She loved it that Sean had come by just to see her again. She had one hand on the door.

"Wait!" Storm cried.

"What?" Annie glanced at the Volkswagen. There were two people in the car. The passenger door opened.

And out stepped Bridget.

4

Annie ducked behind Storm and peeked out. She watched as Bridget closed the passenger door and leaned in the window to say something to Sean. Finally, Bridget turned and started toward the school. But she wheeled around one more time to wave at Sean.

Annie wanted to wipe the smile off her face. "What does she think she's doing? She heard Sean ask me out for Friday."

"Guess she missed the part where he gave you an engagement ring?" Storm offered.

"Thanks for the support, Storm." Annie liked Storm, but, obviously, the girl had never been in love. Otherwise, she couldn't have joked about this. "Bridget's trying to steal my boyfriend, and you don't care?"

"He just gave her a lift, Annie," Storm said.

"Excuse me, girls." Bridget pushed through the doors, giving Annie and Storm her cheerleader smile. "Shouldn't you guys be helping out with homecoming decorations?" She strolled past them and kept going down the hall.

Annie thought of a million comebacks. But she held herself in. *Annie's Rule: Never let the competition see you sweat.*

The library wasn't locked, so Annie figured it was okay to go in. Sometimes kids used the computers to do papers after school, but nobody was there now. Storm had no trouble booting up the computer and logging on to the Net. She went straight to the blog.

Annie forced herself to put Bridget out of her mind. Storm was probably right. It would be just like Bridget to ask Sean for a ride ... and just like kind, unselfish Sean to give her one.

"Annie! Heads up, here," Storm said. "Hamlet's bound to miss us sooner or later. Do you want to read the blog or not?"

Annie pulled up a chair and they scrolled through the site, stopping at Storm's trivia page first:

. . . .
THAT'S WHAT YOU THINK!
by Jane
SEPTEMBER 8

> *DIDYANOSE:*
>
> *Everybody keeps telling us to watch what we eat. But does anybody care about what we call what we eat? Did you know that:*
>
> - *"Caesar" salad is not named after those Roman caesars? There were no salads in those days. Not until the late 1800s did people see fit to eat green leaves. In the 1920s, Caesar Cardini, an Italian immigrant, served the salad that we call by his name, in his Caesar's Restaurant, where famous people hung out.*

- *Cole slaw has nothing to do with coal. "Kohl" is German for cabbage.*
- *Ever wonder why grapefruit has "grape" in it? Not the color, not the taste. It's because grapefruit grow in clusters, like grapes. Who knew?*
- *Did you know that the chocolate kiss has nothing to do with the classic show of affection? I mean, does it look like a kiss to you? Nope. It was named for the hissing sound the chocolate made as it was being spit from the chocolate machine.*

Finally, you deserve to know the truth about sliced bread. A friend of mine thinks this guy we know is the greatest thing since sliced bread. Bet she doesn't know that the sliced sandwich bread wasn't just a good idea — it was a miracle. The sliced loaf was called the "Quiet Miracle" when it came out in 1925, all enriched with vitamins and minerals. Bread helped poor people get rid of crippling and fatal diseases, and even beriberi. So don't be afraid of bread, you carb counters!

Stay tuned for more enlightening information you can easily live without. But let me leave you with this thought. Humans have 46 chromosomes, peas have 14, but the mighty crayfish has 200. Think about it . . .

Annie laughed out loud, and Storm had to shush her. "You're too funny, Storm!" Annie whispered. "You do know that I never said Sean was the greatest thing since sliced bread, right? Sounds like something Granny Lind might say about Gramps. Although now that I think about it, Sean just might be the greatest thing since sliced bread, and way before that."

Storm clicked on Jazz's cartoon to enlarge it. It was a bright blue picture of a Smurf gazing into a mirror while holding his breath. A thought balloon hung above the picture like a cloud. It read: "Wonder what color I'll turn."

Storm laughed hard.

Annie didn't. "Do you think anybody will get it?"

Storm laughed even harder.

"Let's read Grace's blog and get out of here," Annie suggested, reaching over Storm to scroll down to Grace's entry.

• • • • • • • • • • • • • • • • • • • •
THAT'S WHAT YOU THINK!
by Jane
SEPTEMBER 8
SUBJECT: HAMLET

Picture this: Hamlet, the brooding English teacher, a lock of thick sandy-blond hair hanging over one shockingly blue eye. He should be British, wishes he were British, but he is not. He leans against his desk, long legs crossed at the ankles, his Shakespeare in one hand. And he reads Romeo and Juliet *to his class. He's a wonderful reader and a great teacher — don't get me wrong. We're just observing here.*

He pauses. For a second, it's as if he's forgotten he's in front of a room full of sophomores, who are counting the minutes until class is over. He gazes out the window. His lips curve slightly upward and press together. His shoulders relax. His grip on that book tightens. He sighs, deeply, longingly, as his gaze travels up and up. He tilts his head and puts his hand to his cheek.

His head shakes, like he's waking himself from his thoughts. He glances around, as if surprised to see people in the room. "Where was I?" he asks.

Readers, Hamlet is in love! The signs are there.

Stay tuned . . . This could get interesting.

"Hamlet in love? Bridget will be crushed," Storm teased.

"Don't be gross!" Annie said. It was disgusting to think of their English teacher in love. It seemed even weirder than Coach Ramsey getting married. At least with Coach, you couldn't possibly visualize anything remotely romantic.

"So, who do you think the lucky woman is?" Storm asked.

"Lucky? To have Hamlet in love with — "

"Bridget said she saw you two down here." Hamlet stood in the doorway of the library. He was coming toward them, toward the computer. "Well? What are you girls doing in here?"

5

Annie opened her mouth, but nothing came out. She wondered how long Hamlet had been standing there, watching, listening to them. He was just about the last person she'd want to see the *That's What You Think!* blog, especially since Grace's last column was all about him.

Storm clicked madly on the keyboard. "Just shutting down the computer, Mr. Hamilton," she said.

Hamlet reached them just as the screen faded. The little Microsoft tune chimed. "But what were you doing on the computer?" he asked.

Annie was happy to let Storm take the lead. She had no idea how to get out of this without blowing their blog cover. Grace Doe would kill them if they exposed her website.

"Why was the computer on?" Storm began. "Good question! Exactly what I was wondering. But when I saw that it *was* on, I *had* to check my email. I know — I'm sorry. I shouldn't have," Storm babbled. "Seriously, I think I may be addicted to email. And it was like I got these vibes telling me this guy had sent me an email. Really whack, huh? Still, I couldn't stop myself. Must be all that *Romeo and Juliet* we've been reading for class."

Annie glanced up at Mr. Hamilton and wished she had Grace's powers of observation. She couldn't tell if Hamlet was buying Storm's excuse or not. She felt a little sick inside and didn't know if it was because Hamlet wasn't buying into Storm's excuses ... or because he was.

"And did he?" Hamlet asked. "Did he email you?" He seemed so sincere, so understanding, that Annie wanted to confess the whole thing right there.

Storm shook her head and looked disappointed. "You know guys." She took Annie's arm and started past Hamlet, toward the door. "Listen, we're really sorry we can't stay and do the chicken-wire scene. But Annie's mom is expecting her home for dinner."

Annie nodded. She still couldn't speak.

"Ah," he said. "She is?"

"Yeah." Storm kept shoving Annie with her to the library door. "Mrs. Lind specifically told Annie to get home on time."

"Well, go on then," he called after them. "But next time, I expect dedicated chicken-wire labor."

"That was fun," Storm commented once they were safely outside.

"Fun?" Annie repeated. The sun had gone down, and Annie was surprised how dark it was already. "That was so not fun."

Storm shrugged. "What can he do? Ban us from chicken wire for the rest of the year?"

They split in the parking lot. Annie's house was back toward Sam's Sammich Shop, and Storm lived on the other end of town, in the Old West End. By the time Annie reached home, the night had turned chilly.

Before she could open the door, it opened on its own. Mick peeked out. "Hi, Annie!"

"Hey, Mick!" Annie hurried inside, grateful for the warmth and the scent of something spicy and Italian coming from the kitchen. She was grateful to see Mick too. Mom and Annie would have loved to have the Munch over every night, but her parental units limited the Lind dinner night to once a week.

Something about being home helped Annie sense God's presence. It was as if Christ lived in her home. Here, she didn't forget to talk to him. Other voices quieted down, and she could hear his. Annie knew Christ didn't stay in the house when she went to school or to the mall, but sometimes it felt that way. When was she going to learn to walk as closely with God outside these walls as she did inside?

"The shop got really crazy after you left," Mick explained, leading the way to the kitchen. "Your grandparents are so cool. They said they could handle closing without us. They practically kicked us out."

Marbles the Mutt ran out and pounced on Annie, nearly knocking her over. Annie let the big lug lick her chin. "How's my beautiful baby? Did you miss me?"

Mom had rescued Marbles from an animal shelter and given him to Annie on her seventh birthday. They'd both been surprised when the cute little puppy had kept growing and growing into a shaggy gray and white mutt the size of a small horse.

Annie's mom called them into the kitchen, and they sat down to spaghetti, salad, and the best garlic bread in the whole world. Although Annie had watched her weight since the age of five, she cheerfully downed two pieces of the soft, butter-soaked bread. "Storm says sliced bread keeps you from getting diseases," she said, making conversation.

"I've heard that," Mick said, winking at Annie.

Of course she'd heard that. It was straight from Storm's "Didyanose" column. Mick read everything on the blog first since she uploaded for everybody.

"So tell me about homecoming," Mom asked, passing the Parmesan. "Who all's going?"

Annie knew this was her mom's way of asking if Annie had a group date or a "*date* date." "I'm not sure who's going yet," she answered.

"You don't know who you're going with?" Mom sounded surprised, maybe even worried.

Annie couldn't stand for anyone, not even her mother, to think she was such a loser that she couldn't get a date to homecoming. "I'm going with Sean. Sean Davis? He was in the shop today."

Mom nodded, obviously wanting more information.

"He hasn't officially invited me yet."

"Well, I'd love to officially meet him the next time he's in the shop."

"Oh — and I'm meeting him after the game Friday." Mom started to ask a question, but Annie beat her to the answer. "We're meeting at the shop. Good chance for me to officially introduce you."

Mom seemed pleased, or at least appeased. She trailed her garlic bread over her plate, soaking up the last bit of spaghetti sauce. "So ... how are the homecoming decorations coming along?"

Annie groaned. "The decorations are so lame — chicken wire and tissue."

"Like a float?" Mick asked. She sucked in a long strand of spaghetti.

"Exactly," Annie answered. "Jazz had this great idea with lights and shadows, but Bridget and Hamlet wouldn't go for it."

"Annie," her mom said, "do you think it's respectful to call your English teacher Hamlet?"

Annie took the last bite of bread, inhaling the garlic and butter smell. "Hamlet's a pretty cool name for an English teacher, don't you think? Lots better than, say, Macbeth or Dracula, right?"

Her mom sighed.

Mick carried an armload of dishes to the sink. "Thanks again for the great dinner, Sam."

"Yeah. Great dinner, Mom. Thanks." Annie got up from the table. She wanted to call somebody who might still have been at Sam's Sammich Shop when Sean and Bridget left together; somebody who could give her vital information.

Mick! Mick had stayed behind after Annie left. Maybe she'd seen if Bridget had asked Sean for a ride or if he'd offered on his own.

"Hey, Mick? We need to talk."

"Great!" Mick exclaimed. "I'll wash. You dry. It'll only take a minute."

"I'll just stick them in the dishwasher, Mick," Mom offered. "You girls go on up to Annie's room and talk."

Annie led the way to her room. It was small, but Gramps had worked magic in the space, just as he'd done all over their little house. He'd turned a two-bedroom fixer-upper into a cozy, three-bedroom home. Annie's room had a built-in desk along one wall, with storage space underneath. Her closet took up one whole wall. She had her bed under the window, so she could see the moon at night. Granny Lind had made floor-length curtains from kickin' material she had in her attic.

Annie had to agree with her mom that they never would have made it without Granny and Gramps Lind. Her other grandparents, Mom's parents, lived in Florida. Annie loved them too, but they only saw each other once a year.

She plopped on her bed, and Mick took the desk chair.

"Thanks for talking to me, Annie."

That's when she remembered the tryout and the fact that Mick had been trying to talk to her all day. She'd let Mick talk first. Then she'd pump the Munch for information on Sean and Bridget. "Shoot, Munch. Jazz said you're trying out for the boys' team, right?"

"Right. And I'd be really excited about it, except ... except I don't know how to act with all those boys, Annie. They make me so nervous I can't pitch."

Mick was so cute. Annie tried not to smile, though. She could tell how worried the Munch was. "What about Ty? He's your best friend, isn't he?"

"Ty's great. I'm not nervous with him. It's all of the others. Especially guys like Kyle. They think it's a big joke to have me try out with them."

"Kyle Lambert?"

Mick nodded. "It's just ... I get nervous around boys. And I can't be nervous and do my best pitching. I need you to tell me how not to be so nervous. What should I do at practice?"

"Okay. What have you been wearing to practices?"

"Annie!"

"Okay. Okay. Well, try ignoring them. Pretend Ty's the only — "

"Knock-knock." The door wasn't closed. Grace Doe stepped in. "Your mom said to come up. How's it going?"

"Come on in, Grace. Mick and I were just talking about boys."

"About boys' baseball," Mick corrected.

"I keep telling you you'll do great, Mick. I couldn't hit your curve if you paid me," Grace said.

Annie thought it was pretty amazing that Grace and Mick got along so well, especially since Grace didn't get along with that many people, as far as Annie could tell. Grace's dad and Mick's mom had been married about three years. Annie had seen Grace with her half brothers, twin toddlers, and her hunk of an older stepbrother. They sure looked and acted like a family.

Mick fiddled with her ponytail. "Yeah, I'll do just great — as long as I can try out in our backyard, with nobody there except Ty."

"Listen up, you guys," Grace said, staring at the cluster of school photos on Annie's wall. Most of the pictures were from dances or cheerleading. "I've been fielding all the emails that came in for Professor Love after we posted your answers this afternoon. That's why I came by. You better get on these new ones, Annie. Some of them can't wait." She dug out two pages of email printouts from her pocket. "I thought you could read these tonight and come by the cottage tomorrow after school to answer them."

"Grace!" Annie protested. "I can't do this every day. I have commitments."

"I heard," Grace said. "And I understand that nothing comes before chicken wire and tissues. But until things settle down, you need to at least answer the urgent emails, okay?"

Annie's cell went off. She scrambled in her bag for it. "Hello?"

"Hello yourself." The warm, deep voice couldn't have come from anybody else. Sean Davis was on the line.

Annie let herself fall back on her bed and stare at the ceiling. She could almost see Sean's handsome face there. "Is this one of those paid political announcements or something?"

"Annie, it's Sean!" He sounded hurt.

"Sean ..." She trailed it, like she still couldn't figure out who was calling.

"Funny," he said, relaxing now.

"Hey, Annie!" Grace called.

Annie waved the universal "Not now" sign at Grace. To Sean, she said, "So what are you doing?"

Grace sighed so loud Annie was afraid Sean could hear it. She covered the receiver. "Grace, I need to talk here."

Mick had gotten up and moved over to her sister. "Let's give Annie some privacy, Gracie," she suggested.

Annie managed a grateful smile at Mick. The kid was wise beyond her years.

Sean was saying something. " ... when you rushed off today."

She'd missed it, but she couldn't let on. "Well, you know how it goes," she said, hoping that covered it.

Instead of leaving, Grace moved in closer. "Annie," she whispered too loud, "I'll go if you promise to meet me at the cottage after school to answer those emails."

Sean was talking again.

Annie needed to focus on *him*. She nodded at Grace. "Go!" she whispered.

"What?" Sean asked, that hurt creeping back into his voice.

"Not *you*!" Annie cried into the phone. The last thing in the world she wanted was for Sean to go. "Never you, Sean. Never you."

6

Thursday, the day before Annie's first official date with Sean Davis, she still hadn't made it to the cottage to work on the blog emails to Professor Love. She and Grace sat in the back of English class, while Storm held court in the second row. Stephen, Cody, and Bryan seemed to be competing for her attention. Storm Novelo was the center of attention wherever she went. Annie figured Storm wouldn't have any problem getting a date for homecoming. Maybe she already had a date. She hadn't said, and Annie hadn't thought to ask.

Grace wouldn't stop ragging on Annie. "Don't you even care about these desperate people depending on Professor Love? I've tried to answer some of the emails, but there's a bunch nobody but you can handle, Annie."

Annie felt bad. She was pretty sure that the blog was Grace's only social interaction, if you could call hiding behind a computer screen "interaction." "I'm sorry, Grace. It's just with all the cheerleading practices, and this homecoming stuff — "

"Which reminds me — have you started writing that special homecoming article for the blog?" Grace demanded.

Annie felt like tearing her hair out. "One thing at a time, Grace! Okay? I'll answer the love emails. After school. I promise."

"Good. I'll wait for you, and we can walk to the cottage together. Mick's going there after school too."

Hamlet still hadn't started class, thanks to Bridget. She sat front-row center and had their English teacher cornered. Annie strained to hear what she was saying to him.

"You could chaperone!" Bridget was saying. "My parents' house is huge. *Everybody's* coming over after the game. Please come!"

Everybody? Annie thought. This was the first *she'd* heard about it. Annie had gone to one of Bridget's parties when they were freshmen. One was enough. Bridget's parents weren't even there.

"Hey, Annie." Sean slid into the chair next to her, the one she'd managed to save for him by putting her pack on it.

"Nice you could join us, Sean," Mr. Hamilton said. "Why don't you pick up reading in Act 2, Scene 1. Then you can explain the significance of what's occurring there."

Annie passed him her book because it didn't look like he had his with him. She pointed to the right spot, and he started reading. She agonized for him every time he stumbled over a word. Annie glanced at Grace. She was scrawling notes in her observation notebook.

"That's good, Sean," Mr. Hamilton said when Sean got to a stopping place. "Can you explain the background for this action?"

Sean scratched his thick brown hair. "Not exactly."

"How about approximately?" Mr. Hamilton asked.

"Not that either," Sean admitted.

Several kids chuckled, not *at* Sean, but like he'd said something funny on purpose. Annie was grateful for that. Why did Hamlet think he had to show everybody up? Not everybody was into Shakespeare. She'd like to see Hamlet forced to read football plays out of Sean's playbook.

True to her word, Grace was waiting by Annie's locker when school was over. They walked to the cottage together. The sky was gray and depressing. Annie made herself think happier thoughts — like Sean rushing into her arms for a victory hug after tomorrow night's game.

Mick was already there when they reached the cottage. They kicked off their shoes, and Grace turned up the heat. It smelled like lilacs in the living room, for no reason Annie could see.

"How was practice, Mick?" Grace asked. She turned on the computer and waited.

Mick slumped onto the white couch and hugged one of the sofa pillows. "Don't ask." She pulled the pillow over her face.

Annie took a seat on the couch, next to the Munch. "Mick, what happened? It can't be that bad."

Grace sat on the other side of Mick. "You're not off the team, are you?"

Mick punched her pillow. "Not yet. But only because Coach Yardley didn't let anybody go today. They make the cuts next Saturday."

"On homecoming weekend? How unfair is that?" Annie protested.

Mick shrugged.

Annie went on, wanting to joke Mick out of it. "I had Coach Yardley for gym in middle school. He hated having me in class. Seriously! I kept tripping people in soccer. He thought I did it on purpose. Remember, Grace?"

Mick smiled, but it looked forced. Annie didn't think she'd ever seen the Munch this down about anything.

"So what did he say, Mick?" Grace asked.

Mick looked like she was close to crying. "Nothing. But he took me out of the practice game after three batters. I walked one. The other two got hits."

"But it was just practice, right?" Annie asked.

"Yeah. But he must think I'm a lousy pitcher." She turned to Annie. "I did great in warm-ups, when it was just Ty and me, before Coach put me in the game. Kyle was up to bat first. I just felt too weird, like Kyle and all those boys were staring at me. How do you get used to that, Annie?"

Annie wished she had a magic cure. She'd never gotten nervous around guys. She would have loved the guy-girl ratio on Mick's all-boys' team. All she could do was give Mick a hug. "We'll figure it out, Munch. Don't you worry."

Grace logged on to the site. She'd already posted the comments and questions she wanted Annie to answer. All Annie had to do was write in answers.

THAT'S WHAT YOU THINK!
SEPTEMBER 11

Dear Professor Love,

I love my girlfriend, but she drives me crazy! She's always asking me what I'm thinking. Whenever there's a second of silence between us, she smiles up at me and asks, "What are you thinking?" And I want to run away as fast as I can!

— Signed, The Thinking Man — NOT!

Annie cracked her knuckles, then got down to business.

Dear Typical Not-Thinking Man,

How I wish your girlfriend had written me instead of you! I would have shared with her one of Professor Love's Rules: "Never ask a man what he's thinking because he's probably not."

But since you did ask for help, I'll offer these suggestions of what you might answer the next time your girlfriend asks you this threatening question:

"I was thinking how hot your best friend is."

"I've been thinking that all of this outsourcing is a political and cultural nightmare, and yet would it not be a mistake to repeal the NAFTA protocols pertaining to manufactured goods and tariffs?"

"What exactly do you mean by 'thinking'? And 'are'? It depends on what 'are' is."

"Oddly enough, I was sitting here wondering if you haven't put on a few pounds lately. You know, around the hips? Maybe your legs too?"

I guarantee you, she won't ask you that question again. Or anything else.

— Love, Professor Love

Dear Professor Love,

Help! I finally gave in and agreed to go on a blind date out to dinner. Now I'm scared that I'll hate the guy and won't be able to end the date fast enough. What can I do??

— Not Blind Enough

Dear Not Blind Enough,

Not to worry. Follow these instructions, and you'll be home before dark:

Bring crayons in your purse, and color on the placemat and tablecloth while waiting for your food.

Bring a book and read it while you're eating . . . and he's talking.

Throughout the evening, show your teeth and stare, fascinated, at his neck.

Whistle at cute guys at other tables.

Ask the waiter if they have any live food.

While he's talking, do a little pantomime act — as if there's an invisible window between you and him.

Sing in public. Poorly. Preferably something cheesy and disco or just theme songs to stupid TV shows.

If none of these things work, then it's time to rethink the situation. You may have been lined up with a guy who will be loyal to you, no matter what!

— Love, Professor Love

Annie quickly answered four more emails. She wished she had more time to spend on it.

When she finished, she turned the computer over to Mick. "It's all yours, Munch," she said, putting on her jacket. "Don't worry about those old baseball boys either. We'll think of something, okay?"

"Thanks, Annie," Mick said, taking her seat in front of the screen. She read Annie's answers, then commented, "Man, I wish I had a fraction of the answers you have for guys."

"You will, Munch," Annie said. She glanced at the grandfather clock in the corner. If it was right, Storm would be at Sam's Sammich Shop right now, waiting for her. "Grace, I'm done!" she hollered.

Grace came in from the kitchen. "You're kidding. You answered all the love emails already?"

"Yup. And I think even you will be pleased. But I gotta jet. Storm's waiting for me at the shop. Why don't you guys meet us over there as soon as you can? We'll celebrate another successful week of *That's What You Think!* Ice cream on the house. Mick's flavor." Mick had invented her own flavor of ice cream, and Annie's mom said they'd been selling quite a bit of "Ice Cream à la Mick."

"Cool," Grace agreed. "I'm in. I'll call Jazz and see if she can meet us over there."

Mick looked up from the screen. "I told Sam I'd help out tonight, so I'm headed there anyway."

Annie had to get going. Storm didn't like to be kept waiting. She moved to the door. "Great! See you later then! Bye."

Annie walked as fast as she could without sweating. It wasn't just Storm she was thinking about. There was a good chance Sean would drop by the shop. That, she didn't want to miss!

As she got close to Sam's Sammich Shop, Annie smoothed her hair and tried to check herself in the store windows she passed. At the door of the shop, she took a deep breath, smiled, and made her entrance. She glanced around, hoping to see Sean.

Instead, there, sitting at the counter and eating ice cream like a normal person, was Hamlet.

7

Annie stared at the back of Holden Hamilton's sandy-blond head. What was he doing here at her mother's sandwich shop? It was bad enough she had to deal with him at Big Lake High. Not here! But there he sat, chatting with Mom as if he were a regular person. Was he reporting on her? Tattling to her mother?

"Annie!" Mom waved her over. "Hi, honey. How was everything at school?"

Annie thought about her answer. Maybe it was a trick question. Who knew what Hamlet had already said about Annie's life at school? "About the same," she answered carefully.

"Hello, Annie," Hamlet said.

Annie knew that if she didn't stop thinking of him as "Hamlet," sooner or later that's what she'd call him to his face. "Hello, Mr. Hamilton."

They exchanged forced smiles for an awkward moment. Then he asked, "Were you working on homecoming decorations?"

"No, but I've been there all week," she answered defensively. "I had something I had to do after school."

"I needed a break too," he said, smiling. Actually smiling. Annie had learned a long time ago that all teachers came with two faces — one for their students, and one for parents.

Neither of them said anything else, and the silence grew awkward.

"Well," Annie's mom said, glancing from one to the other, "I'm sure all that hard work will pay off. You'll have a wonderful homecoming."

Thankfully, Storm walked up. And as always, everybody's attention was drawn to her. "Greetings, all! Annie, we're over there." She nodded toward the back.

Annie jumped at the chance to break away. "Well, Storm and I have to . . . you know. Anyway . . ." She backed away, then followed Storm to a table, where Jazz was sitting, knotting straw wrappers into chains worthy of necklaces.

"Weird, huh?" Storm whispered.

Annie eased herself into a chair, keeping her back to Hamlet.

"You don't look so hot," Jazz commented.

"Why would he come here?" Annie asked.

"Who?" Jazz said.

"Him!" She jerked her head toward the counter. "My English teacher!"

"Ummm," Jazz began, "for ice cream? Maybe a sandwich?"

"Or," Storm offered, her eyes getting big, "maybe he read Gracie's blog about him and he's come for revenge!" She said the last word like it was a cliff-hanger to a scary movie before a commercial break.

Fifteen minutes later, Mick and Grace showed up. Grace turned her chair around and straddled it backward. "What's Hamlet doing here?"

"Ask Annie," Jazz suggested. "She's got dozens of theories."

Annie risked a glance over her shoulder. Hamlet was reading the shop's copy of the *Big Lake News*. "There should be a law against teachers hanging out in student hangouts."

Mick disappeared to the kitchen, and Grace fell into a conversation with Jazz and Storm about the blog. Annie couldn't follow it. She had too much on her mind.

After a while, Grace turned to Annie. "Annie, what do you really know about Sean?"

The question took her by surprise. "What do you mean?"

Grace eyed her. "I mean, besides the general consensus that he's not entirely bad-looking and that he plays football, what do you know about him?"

Annie felt like she should defend Sean. "He's a good guy, Grace. You just don't know him."

"Like you do?" Grace countered.

Annie knew what Grace was getting at. In their youth group at church, they'd talked a lot about dating and how the most important thing about a guy was his walk with the Lord.

Storm broke in. "Ease up, Grace. Coach Ramsey is the one getting married. Annie here just wants a date."

But Annie knew it didn't work like that. Girls married guys they dated. And they became like guys they dated.

"Here comes ice cream!" Jazz said, obviously eager to change the subject.

Mick reappeared with a tray of "Ice Cream à la Mick." She
served everybody, then pulled up a chair. "What's up with
your mom and grandparents?"

"What do you mean?" Annie asked. Her mind was still
coming up with answers to Grace's questions about Sean.

"I've just never seen them like this before." Mick handed
everybody a napkin.

"Like what?"

Mick shrugged. "You can cut the atmosphere back there
with a knife. It's not so much what they're saying — more like
what they're not saying."

"You've got to be wrong, Mick." The only time Annie had
ever seen her grandparents and her mom argue was when
they were trying to out-nice each other: "*You* go home. I'll
take care of the shop." "No. *You* go home. I'll do it."

Some seniors in the back booth yelled at Mick to get their
drinks, and she hurried back to the kitchen.

Annie glanced over at the counter again. Hamlet was gone.
She didn't see her mom or her grandparents. Mick had to be
wrong, though. Mom was so close to Granny and Gramps
that she couldn't have lasted two minutes if they'd been mad
at each other. She was the same way with Annie.

"Ty told me about Mick's practice today," Jazz said. "I'd
like to string those guys up by their toes."

"Nice image," Storm commented.

"Possible website cartoon, Jazz," Grace suggested.

"So what did those little middle-school fellows do?" Storm
asked.

Jazz filled Storm in on Mick's trouble with the guys' team.
Kyle had been more obnoxious than ever, and Mick's pitches

to him had been wilder than ever. When Jazz finished the details, she glanced over at Mick, who was wiping off tables. "I just wish we could do something to help."

So did Annie. She couldn't stand the thought of Mick being disappointed.

Storm scraped the last bite of Ice Cream à la Mick from her dish. "When's the next practice?"

"Tomorrow afternoon," Grace answered.

Jazz was still stirring her ice cream into peaks and dips, sculpting instead of eating. "Ty said I could go watch."

"We should all go!" Annie exclaimed. She loved the idea of surprising Mick, showing up and putting those guys in their places.

"That would be so tight!" Grace agreed. "Let's — "

Annie stopped listening. Sean was walking toward them. Her stomach knotted as she watched him come straight to her table.

"Hey, Annie. Ladies." Sean put his hand on the back of Annie's chair, but he shared his smile with all of them. "Coach Ramsey was a slave driver today. Thought I'd get some energy food. You busy, Annie?"

Annie smiled up at him, then glanced at her friends, hoping they'd understand. "We're about done, aren't we?" She got to her feet.

"What are we?" Grace muttered. "Chopped liver?"

Annie couldn't help but hear her. She just hoped Sean hadn't heard it too. Annie needed to spend time with Sean. Grace herself had accused Annie of not knowing him very well. Maybe this was her chance.

Sean downed two Sam Burgers and fries, while he explained to her the team strategy for Friday night's game. She loved listening to the sound of his voice, even if all he talked about was football plays. She waited patiently for the right moment to turn the conversation, but it just didn't come.

His plate empty, Sean leaned back in the booth. "Coach keeps talking about his wedding. I wish he hadn't made us be his ushers. I'm going to feel stupid."

"What are you talking about? You will be totally rockin' in your little usher suit." Annie could picture herself on Sean's arm, being escorted down the sideline.

"Well, I better get home," Sean said, sliding out of the booth and tossing his napkin onto his empty plate. "Coach says we need a good night's sleep before the game tomorrow."

Annie was surprised to see the shop had cleared and the lights were dimmed. She followed him to the door. "I'm looking forward to tomorrow night, Sean. Want me to wait for you at the lockers after the game?" She was thinking that their date would look more official if she rode over with him, instead of meeting him at the shop.

Sean shrugged. "Coach'll keep us in the locker room for his little after-game talk. We can just meet up here later."

Annie kept her disappointment to herself. *Don't care more than he does — Annie's Rule.* "Cool. See you tomorrow!"

"Okay. Bye." Sean Davis stuck his hands into the pockets of his letter jacket and left.

Annie closed the door and ducked around so she could watch from the window as he drove away.

Voices came from the kitchen.

She started to go back there, then stopped.

"Can we please talk about it?" Annie's mom sounded close to tears.

"There's no need, Sam," Gramps said. "It's none of our business."

"'Night, Sam," Granny said, her voice so strained that it barely sounded like her.

Granny and Gramps pushed through the double doors and almost crashed into Annie.

"Granny?" Annie had never seen her grandmother look so ... so hurt. Gramps' face was blank. "Gramps, what's the matter?"

He tried to smile at her but couldn't quite pull it off. "Didn't see you there, honey. Nothing's the matter. Your grandma's just tired. That's all. You have a good night now." He put his arm around Granny, then brushed past Annie and out the door.

"'Night, Annie," Gran called back.

Something was way wrong.

"Annie? What are you still doing here?" Mom turned out the overhead light.

"What's wrong with Granny and Gramps?"

Mom shook her head. "Nothing. I mean, it's all so silly. I think they'll be fine in the morning, once they've had a chance to think things through."

"Think what things through?"

Mom got out her keys and motioned Annie to step outside so she could lock the door. "They're blowing everything out of proportion."

Outside, Annie waited while her mother turned the key and put it back into her purse. "So? What're they blowing out of proportion?"

Mom heaved a sigh. "This is not a big deal, Annie." She paused, as if she were sorting through words to get to the right ones. "Oh, all right. I'm ... I'm going out with somebody. It's not even a date. It's more like ... like friends going to the same place together." She headed for the car.

Annie followed, but her legs were on automatic pilot. Thoughts circled in her head, refusing to land. Her mother was going out with somebody? She'd never done that before. Annie had always felt that her father was the kind of man her mother would never get over.

Annie would have given anything to have her dad back right now.

They rode home in silence.

Marbles raced from one to the other when they got home. Even he seemed to pick up on the tension between them.

Annie went straight to her room and tried to finish her homework. But she couldn't concentrate. Who could "Somebody" be? She wasn't about to ask Mom. Mentally, she did an inventory of the regulars who came into the shop, but she had to stop because each guess made her feel like throwing up. Her mom. And a man. There was nothing wrong with it, of course. Part of her believed her mother deserved to date after all these years. But another part of her didn't want there to be anybody but Johnny Lind, ever.

Without even realizing what she was doing, Annie started praying. *Father, I don't know why I feel like this. Am I just being selfish? I don't want to be. Help me to see what's going on through*

*your eyes. Mom probably needs me to be happy for her, or at least to
be okay. I'm going to need you to change me inside so I can do that.
Because I'm not okay. I'm totally un-okay.*

She wanted to talk it through with somebody else before
facing Mom again. Not Granny and Gramps. Obviously, they
were as mixed up about this as she was. She couldn't talk to
Sean about it because she didn't know what he'd think. Storm
wouldn't understand. Her parents had always been together.
Same story with Jazz. Annie thought of her other friends at
school. Megan's parents were divorced, and her mother dated
more than Megan did. But Megan never talked about God.
She'd get the part about dating, but not the part about Annie
wanting God to help her through this mess.

Then she thought of Grace. Grace had been so upset when
her dad married Mick's mom that she hadn't even gone to the
wedding. Grace liked Lisa now, but she must have hated it
when her dad started dating. Maybe Grace would understand
what Annie was feeling.

Annie checked her phone file on her cell and found Grace's
number.

Grace answered on the fourth ring. "Annie? What's up?"

The words spilled out in spurts and stops. Grace kept quiet
while Annie got it all out — the strain between her mom and
grandparents, Mom admitting that she was going out with
somebody, Annie's own mixed-up feelings. "Grace, how did
you handle it when your dad started dating?"

"You're asking the wrong person, Annie. Unless you want
to learn by my mistakes. I was so mad. I didn't talk to Dad
for weeks. I left pictures of my mom everywhere when I knew
he'd be bringing Lisa home. She was the only one he dated.

It's weird. I knew Mom was dating like a jillion guys, and I handled that okay. But with Dad, it was harder. Maybe it's worse when there's just one other person."

"Maybe," Annie agreed.

"And it's got to be even worse for you. At least I didn't have to see Lisa every day at school."

"What do you mean?"

"Lisa wasn't a teacher or anything," Grace said. "Hey, and don't worry. No more Hamlet columns. But you gotta know that I didn't know about your mom when I wrote that stuff."

"What?" Annie was getting a sick feeling in her stomach.

"I hadn't seen them together until tonight. I admit I suspected something right off, but I didn't want to say anything until you did."

Annie's head felt dizzy. "What a minute, Grace. What are you saying?"

Grace was quiet for a minute. "Annie, I thought you knew. I'm sorry. Man, you shouldn't have called me! You know I never say the right thing."

Annie held her breath. Her heart pounded against her chest. "Tell me, Grace. Who's my mom going out with?"

Then Grace said it. "Hamlet."

8

Friday morning, Annie should have been cloud-floating. Tonight would be her first official date with Sean. But instead of floating, Annie felt as if she were sinking deeper and deeper. And all she wanted to do was pull the covers over her head and go back to sleep.

Hamlet and her mom! How could this be happening?

But it *was* happening. Annie threw back the covers and started getting ready, deciding that the best way to handle the morning was to get out of the house fast. She couldn't face her mom. Not yet. She showered, put on her cheerleading uniform, slapped on makeup, and raced downstairs and straight for the front door.

She'd almost made it when her mom rushed out from the kitchen. "Annie, what are you doing? You haven't eaten breakfast."

Annie couldn't bring herself to look at her mother. She fidgeted with her backpack. "Not hungry."

"I was going to let you drive. I have a doctor's appointment this morning. You can use the practice, if you're going to pass the driving test next month."

"Thanks, Mom. But I'd rather walk this morning." Annie reached for the doorknob.

"Okay. That's enough. We have to talk."

Annie braced herself. She wasn't ready to talk.

Mom walked up to her. "Honey, you're making a big a deal out of nothing."

"You're the one who's always telling me that dating *is* a big deal." It was out before she could stop it.

"This isn't even a date!" Mom protested.

"Okay. Let me get this straight. You're going out, but it isn't a date. I'll have to remember that one next time *I* want to go out."

"Annie, it's not the same thing, and you know it."

"Then why couldn't you have this *un-date* with somebody who's *not* my English teacher?" Annie could tell that one hit dead center.

"Who told you ... ?" Mom stopped and seemed to regroup. "Holden ... Mr. Hamilton ... and I are just friends. He comes into the shop sometimes."

Annie didn't say anything. *Annie's Rule: Silence is a powerful weapon.*

Mom went on. "Anyway, somehow the subject of homecoming came up, and we got to talking about the dance and how hard that was going to be to chaperone, and he just kind of asked if I'd go with him. To help."

"Homecoming?" This was surreal. Her English teacher had asked her mother to homecoming? What was this, a soap opera? "This is just great," she said, picking up her backpack. "My mother has a date to homecoming, and I don't."

Grace was waiting for Annie when she got to her locker. "You okay?" she asked. "I didn't mean to get you upset last night. I really thought you knew about your mom and ... you know."

Annie knew it took a lot for Grace Doe to apologize about anything. "It's okay, Grace. It's not your fault that my mom's going to homecoming with my English teacher." Her locker didn't open, so she kicked it and tried again.

"No way," Grace said. "Homecoming? What are you going to do?"

The locker opened with a *clunk*. Annie threw books in and pulled books out. "Do? Well, since at this point I don't have a date, there's not much *to* do."

"I thought you were going with Sean Davis."

"I don't know. We're meeting after the game tonight." She slammed the locker. "I was pretty sure I could get him to ask me to homecoming tonight. Now I'm not sure about anything."

"I know I hassled you about Sean, Annie. It's just ... well, you definitely know how to pick the cutest guys in school. I'm just not sure you always get the *right* guys. You deserve someone who wants and likes the same things you do, you know? Hey, don't forget. You're Professor Love." Grace glanced away, but Annie could see her cheeks were red. "I'll shut up now."

Annie had to grin. This was the most Grace had ever talked to her, at least about anything personal. "I don't want you to shut up, okay? Thanks ... Gracie."

Gracie's face broke into a grin. She really was pretty, especially when she smiled. "I don't think you've ever called me 'Gracie.'" Annie's gaze took in Gracie's camouflage T-shirt, her black jeans and high-top sneakers. A couple of weeks ago, Annie barely knew Grace Doe. Yet right now she felt closer to Gracie than to any of her cheerleading friends. "Gracie fits," she said.

The day dragged on. Annie dreaded sixth hour, when she'd have to face Hamlet. She waited until the last minute before class, then slipped in next to Gracie on the back row. Gracie's observation notebook was open, and she was scribbling. Annie saw "shined shoes" and "new shirt" before Gracie slapped the book shut.

"Sorry," Gracie said. "I won't use any of it. I just can't help myself taking notes, though."

Annie shrugged. It didn't matter. Next week, at the homecoming dance, the whole world would know that her mother and Hamlet ... she couldn't even finish the thought.

Storm strolled in late. Even though she was only a freshman, she took English and history with the sophomores. She had science with the juniors. "Greetings," she said, plopping next to Annie. She acted so normal, at least normal for Storm, that Annie was pretty sure she didn't know about Hamlet yet. Good for Gracie keeping it a secret. At least for now.

"Bridget would like to make an announcement about homecoming," Hamlet said.

Bridget stood up and faced the class from the front row. "We need all of you to get in the Big Lake High spirit!" she exclaimed.

"Is this a cheer?" Storm asked.

Bridget looked confused. "No. Uh — we have a lot of work to do on homecoming decorations. As chairwoman, I want to invite all of you to come and help us after school. I've been working so hard!" Bridget faked a pouty look and held up one hand. "See? I broke two fingernails on chicken wire!"

Storm piped up. "Whoa! It takes six months to grow a fingernail, base to tip. Thought the class should be aware of the risks involved in tissue art."

Bridget took her seat.

It was the only bright spot in Annie's otherwise rotten day.

Cheerleading practice was lousy. Annie couldn't get anything right. Her big feet felt like clown feet. And Bridget was quick to point out every mistake.

As Annie was leaving practice, she overheard Bridget talking with one of the senior cheerleaders. "You should come over after the game," she was saying. "Everybody will be there."

Annie couldn't help feeling hurt that Bridget hadn't invited her, especially since *everybody* would be there. She didn't have any desire to take Sean to one of Bridget's parties, but it would have been nice to be asked. She told herself that everything was fine. She had to forget about Bridget, forget about Hamlet and her mother, forget about everything except Sean. She and Sean were about to have their first real date. And she needed her focus back. Tonight was the night for the final stage of Operation Sean.

There was no way her mother was going to the
homecoming dance and she wasn't.

Annie cheered herself hoarse at the football game. Sean
caught two passes, and Stephen made an interception. But the
game was scoreless at halftime, when the cheerleaders led the
crowd in the wave, then cheered into a pyramid.

Things fell apart for Big Lake in the second half. They
couldn't make a first down in the third quarter, and the
fourth quarter was even worse. The team lost, 17 to 0. Annie
wanted to run after Sean and tell him it was okay, that he had
done a great job. But Coach Ramsey rounded up the players
in the locker room, and everybody knew the guys wouldn't
come out until he was done with them.

"Hey!" Storm walked out onto the field, where Annie was
still standing, staring after Sean and the others. Storm was
wearing knee-high, high-heeled leather boots and a leather
miniskirt. She picked her way across the dirt clods to Annie.
"You look cold."

Annie realized she was shivering. The night had gotten
colder, and her cheerleading uniform didn't help much. "I was
hoping to talk to Sean."

"I thought you were meeting him at the shop."

"I am." She gazed across the empty football field. "I just feel
so awful for him."

"You can feel awful for him where it's warm. Come on.
Cody can give you a lift."

"Cody?"

Storm shrugged. "Yup. Cody. Come on. We're off to Sam's Sammich Shop!" She linked arms with Annie, and Annie let herself be led off the field, to Cody's old Ford Galaxy.

Cody sat behind the wheel, the motor running, and the heater, thankfully, blasting hot air. Annie climbed in back.

"Seat belts, everybody!" Storm commanded. "Don't make me pull out safety statistics."

At first, Annie felt weird, like a third shoe, size 9 1/2. But by the time Cody pulled into the parking lot of Sam's Sammich Shop, they were all laughing together.

"Thanks for the ride, Cody," Annie said, kicking aside the fast-food trash scattered on the floor of his car. "But you really ought to clean up back here. If I get some horrible disease, I'll know who to blame."

"Are you kidding?" Cody said, shutting off the engine. "Storm says every square inch of the human body has about thirty-two million bacteria on it. You're probably giving my car a horrible disease."

Inside the shop, kids were already filling the tables and booths. "I'll get us a booth in back!" Cody yelled over the Beach Boy music.

Once they were by themselves, Annie asked Storm, "Why didn't you tell me you had a date with Cody?"

"It's not exactly a date. We just met up at the game. We're going to homecoming together, though."

Annie grabbed Storm's arm. "Get out! You and Cody?" She was happy for both of them. Really. Still, something gnawed at her inside. She recognized it as jealousy, which was stupid. She and Cody were just friends. They always had been. She couldn't have picked a better date for Storm. But admitting that tiny bit of jealousy made her feel like a crummy friend. Annie bet Mick never felt jealous of her friends.

"Wow! That's so tight!" Annie exclaimed, determined to be totally happy for Storm.

Storm shrugged it off, but Annie could tell she was pleased. "Cody's okay. Can you believe he remembered that thirty-two-million-bacteria thing?"

"You better go sit with him before Bridget notices how cute he is," Annie warned. She was kidding. Anyway, Bridget was probably home having her big party for *everybody*.

Mick charged out of the kitchen with a tray full of food. Annie scooted out of her way. "Hey, Mick! How's it going? Need any help?"

"We got it. Thanks. Too bad about the game." Mick shifted the tray. "I better get this stuff delivered. See you later."

Annie thought about helping out. Game nights could get pretty busy. Her mom never made her work when she was with friends. Still, if she hadn't been so mad about Hamlet, she might have pitched in. Instead, she wandered through the shop to check who was there. She exchanged game talk with a couple of tables. Everybody was pretty bummed about the loss.

"Annie!" Storm called from the very back booth, the one under the picture of Paul McCartney on one side and the mural of the Beach Boys on the other. "Come on over!"

It was nice of Storm to try to include her, but Annie didn't want to get in the way. "That's okay, Storm!" she called back.

"Don't be whack!" Storm shouted. "Get over here!"

Annie guessed it would be okay. Cody and Storm were sitting across from each other, so she slid in next to Storm. "Thanks. Sean should be here pretty soon."

"Hey," Storm replied. "I'm glad to capitalize on these rare moments of Sean's absence, when I can actually spend some time with you."

Annie wanted to defend herself, even though Storm didn't look angry. Annie loved her friends. It was just that she was in the middle of Operation Sean. Storm should understand that. "I don't see Sean that often, Storm."

Storm raised her hand in "Stop" mode. "Whoa, girl. Just kidding here."

Cody changed the subject.

"I wouldn't want to be in that locker room now," Cody said. He ran track in the spring, but didn't play football or basketball.

"I just hope Coach doesn't keep them too long," Annie said, glancing up at the clock.

For the next hour, Annie tuned in and out of the conversation between Storm and Cody. Every time the door slammed open, she hopped up to see if it was Sean. "This is crazy!" she complained. "Even for Ramsey."

"Maybe Sean went home first," Cody suggested, "to change or something?"

"I'm sure he's just trapped in that locker room while Coach takes out his frustrations and pre-wedding jitters on the team," Annie complained.

Cody glanced at Storm and looked at his hands.

"What?" Annie asked. Something was going on between them.

"Annie, look around," Storm said. "I don't even know all the football players, but I've seen a couple of guys I know are on the team."

Annie had been looking so hard for Sean, she'd hardly registered anybody else. Now that she looked, she saw Jon, Michael, Jason, TJ, and Jared, BLHS's star quarterback, who'd had a lousy game.

So where was Sean?

She forced herself to smile and make small talk with Cody and Storm. Mick brought fries and onion rings and Cokes. Any minute now, Sean would rush through the door, looking for her.

After another half hour went by, Annie couldn't take it anymore. "Excuse me," she said, sliding out of the booth. She made her way to Michael's table. She and Michael had sort of gone out at the beginning of the year, before Sean.

"Hey, Margo," she said, aiming a warm smile at Michael's date. "Michael, you guys played a good game. Bad breaks all around."

"Tell me about it," Michael said.

"Did you see Sean after the locker-room pow wow?" she asked, trying to play it casual.

"Sean? I don't know. He left before I did."

Annie tried to hide the rage that was building inside. "Okeydoke. Good to know."

Annie had no idea where Sean was. But he wasn't here. And that meant one thing.

For the first time in her life, Annie Lind had been stood up.

9

"Annie, are you okay?" Mick asked.

Annie didn't know how long she'd been standing at the window, gazing into the parking lot of Sam's Sammich Shop, fuming at the very idea that she had been stood up. She glanced down at Mick, who was putting on her Indians jacket, obviously getting ready to leave. "What?"

"You've been standing there forever," Mick said. "Everything all right? I was worried about you."

"Mick, beware of love," she said, fighting off the hurt and fanning it into pure anger. "Guys can be so ... so ... so *guys*!"

"I don't know about love," Mick admitted. "But I know I don't understand guys."

"Oh, I understand them all right. And the next time I see Sean Davis, he's going to understand me!" She imagined Sean walking in right now. He wouldn't know what hit him. She wished her dad were alive. Johnny Lind would make Sean sorry.

"Mom's coming to get me," Mick said, moving toward the door. "You want a ride?"

"That'd be great. Yeah. Thanks, Mick." Annie glanced at the kitchen. She definitely didn't want a ride from her mother.

"Your grandpa showed up," Mick said. "Did you see him?"

Annie shook her head. But she was glad he was there. She understood why he was so upset with Mom, but she couldn't stand to see them acting so weird.

"He slipped in the back door," Mick explained. "I don't think he and your mom have even spoken to each other. It makes me so sad. I just don't get it."

"You'd understand if you knew what Granny and Gramps know about Mom."

Mick held the shop door open, and they stepped outside under a black, cloudy sky. "You mean because she's going out with Mr. Hamilton?" Mick asked.

"Great," Annie mumbled. "Does the whole world know?"

Mick shrugged. "Your dad's been gone a long time, Annie. Your grandparents know how much your mom loved him. But I'll bet Sam gets lonely. She's so busy with the shop. I'll bet she doesn't get away much."

Annie should have known Mick would take Mom's side.

A yellow Volkswagen, going too fast, pulled into the gravel lot and parked crooked. Annie watched, her fingernails digging into the palms of her clenched fists, as Sean got out with Stephen and Jon, a junior halfback. They were laughing and slapping each other on the back as if they'd won tonight.

Annie stood her ground. Sean was going to have to walk right past her. She searched her mind for appropriate "Annie's Rules." *The tongue is mightier than the sword. Guys treat you the way you allow them to treat you.*

"Hey, Annie!" Sean waved, as if he weren't two hours late. "You didn't have to wait outside for me."

Annie didn't answer, but she knew the glare she was giving him said more than words.

"Oooh. Careful, Sean," Jon warned. "I see flames coming out of those nostrils. What did you do, guy?"

"Don't ask me," Sean said, palms up. "Annie, how come you're not talking?"

Was it possible he didn't know how mad she'd be? Could he be that dense?

"Annie," Mick whispered, "my mom's here."

Annie hadn't released Sean from her stare.

Sean glanced at his watch as if he had no idea it was so late. "Okay. I'm late. Sorry. But that was a really hard game we lost."

Stephen and Jon mumbled their agreement.

"You lost a lot more than a game, Sean," Annie said coolly.

A horn beeped.

"Annie?" Mick called.

Stephen and Jon walked on into the shop, leaving Sean to fend for himself.

"Come on, Annie," Sean coaxed. He put his hand on her shoulder, and she shook it off.

"You, Sean Davis," she said sweetly, "are a total waste of makeup."

"Huh?"

"I know that I have to date a few bad guys so that I'll appreciate the good guys. But I had you in the wrong group … until tonight. Thanks for clearing that up." She turned to go with Mick.

"Annie!"

Annie kept walking. Mick trotted ahead to her mom's car. Annie could see Gracie in the backseat. She had to hold herself together. *Never let the guy see how deeply he hurt you ... unless such knowledge can be used to your advantage — Annie's Rule.*

"Annie, please!" Sean cried.

Mick hopped into the backseat with Gracie and said something to her mom. Annie walked to the passenger side. Tears burned in her throat. She'd really believed this might be the beginnings of love, what she and Sean were feeling.

"Annie! Don't leave!" Sean pleaded.

Annie had one hand on the door handle.

"Annie, I was going to ask you to homecoming!" he shouted.

Annie stopped.

"Will you? Will you go to homecoming with me, Annie?"

Annie looked across the parking lot to where Sean was standing under a streetlight. In his letter jacket, he was so husky, so strong. And here he was, pleading with her, begging her. Her head was pounding, ready to explode. She couldn't think.

"Come back, Annie! Please?"

Annie felt her heart soften. She didn't want to stay mad at him. She wanted something to go right in her life. "Where were you tonight, Sean?" She waited for an answer. In the back of her mind, she heard Bridget bragging about her party: *Everybody will be there.*

Was Sean part of "everybody"? Did he go without her because he knew she wouldn't go? "I'm waiting!" she shouted.

Sean waved his hands in the air. "We just drove around to blow off steam. That's all. Come on, Annie!"

She wanted to believe him. She needed something in her world to make sense, to end happily ever after.

"Annie, are you coming?" Mick's mom asked.

"Yeah. Get in!" Gracie demanded from the backseat.

She couldn't leave him. This was what she'd worked for, wasn't it? She'd done everything she could think of to get Sean Davis to ask her to homecoming. Now he had. He deserved a chance, didn't he? Didn't *they*? "Umm ... I ... Thanks, Mrs. Doe. I guess I don't need a ride after all."

Annie watched the car drive out of the parking lot, with Gracie staring intently at her through the rear window. Then she walked, slowly, conscious of the eyes upon her, across the parking lot and into the arms of the hottest guy in Big Lake.

Annie slept in so late on Saturday that she had to hurry to get dressed by noon. Her mom had left a note on the kitchen table, saying that she was at the shop. The note was more communication than they'd had in days. Annie missed her mom. It would have been nice to talk to her about Sean. After he'd asked her to homecoming, he couldn't have been sweeter. They'd talked until curfew, when Sean had driven her home. But she still had her doubts. She wanted to believe him, to trust him, but she didn't know if she could. Gracie was right. Annie had to admit that she still didn't know Sean that well.

Annie walked to Big Lake Foods and caught Storm and Gracie at the end of their shift. Then they headed for the mall to look for homecoming dresses.

"So, last night worked out okay, I guess?" Storm asked as they crossed Jackson Street at a trot. "Have to admit that Cody and I were surprised to see you walk back in with Sean. He must have done some fancy apologizing."

Annie didn't answer directly. Had he? Apologized? He must have. She'd been so mad. "He came through with the homecoming invite."

"Sweet!"

Gracie didn't say anything, but the look she shot Annie did. She was not pleased. Annie didn't want to get into it. She turned to Storm. "You need a homecoming dress too, right?"

"Fasheezy," Storm said. "Although I doubt if they carry my style at the Big Lake mall. Gracie and I are here for moral support only."

The sun wasn't shining, but it was warmer than Annie expected as they cut through the campus of Big Lake University. She was surprised to see so many leaves turning already. A red-orange maple leaf floated in front of her, and she reached out and caught it. It would be a great color for a homecoming dress, she decided, tucking the leaf into her jacket pocket.

"Storm, did you see all that food the Lazarro sisters bought for Coach's wedding reception?" Gracie asked.

"Yeah," Storm answered. "Are you going?"

"Mick's got tryouts that afternoon, and I promised I'd go watch," Gracie said. "But I could still make the wedding. Might be some good observations there. Blogging material."

They hit every store in the mall. Annie tried on twenty-three dresses before going back to the first store and buying the first dress she'd tried on. It was strapless, red-orange, with tiny stars in swirling stripes. They voted, and it was unanimous. It left $3.93 in her checking account.

They hurried back to the cottage. Annie felt ridiculous carrying her dress with her, but she didn't want to risk leaving it at the store. She could leave it at the cottage, and maybe Sean would drive her over to pick it up later. It would be a good excuse to see him again.

By the time they reached the cottage, Annie was whacked out. Her arm throbbed from carrying the dress.

Jazz and Mick were waiting for them.

"Let me see," Jazz demanded, unzipping the hanger bag. She and Mick peered in.

"It's beautiful, Annie!" Mick exclaimed. "You'll look so pretty in that."

"Good colors," Jazz said, ever the artist. Annie considered it high praise, coming from Jazz. "How about you, Storm? Aren't you going to homecoming with the track guy?"

"Cody," Storm said. "He's wearing a vintage tux he borrowed from his great-uncle. I'm going Roaring '20s. I've got the shawl; gold, of course. Still hunting for that perfect fringed flapper dress, though."

"That's so tight!" Jazz exclaimed. "If I ever go to one of these things, that's the way I'll do it. One-of-a kind wardrobe."

It was the most positive Annie had ever heard Jazz, and she couldn't help feeling a little jealous. Jazz was more excited about Storm's nonexistent dress than she was about the one Annie had just spent her life's savings on.

"We better get started," Mick said. "I've got practice at four."

Annie felt a pang of guilt. She hadn't been much help with Mick's boy problems. "Hey, Munch, want me to come to your practice?"

"Are you kidding? That would be great! It's just a practice, though. Homecoming Saturday's when Coach makes the cuts."

Annie tugged on Mick's cap. "How could anybody cut you, Mick? You're way too cute."

For the next few minutes, they talked about where they wanted the blog to go. Annie knew it wasn't easy for Gracie to let anybody else have a say in the website. It had all been her idea, her blog. But the site had grown into something bigger. It belonged to all of them, and Gracie was doing okay with that.

Mick pulled up the website, and they all oohed and aahed over Jazz's new and improved graphics. Gracie had quit blogging about Hamlet, thankfully, and had come up with some cool observations about "couples." She scrolled through the site, then took control of the meeting. "Storm, I still need your next trivia column. Annie, you're doing the article on homecoming, right?"

"Which should be easier, now that you actually have a date to homecoming," Storm teased.

"There are a couple of love emails you should do before you leave today," Gracie added.

Annie groaned. She didn't feel like being Professor Love this afternoon.

Gracie forced Storm to scrawl some trivia food facts in longhand, while Jazz watched and laughed. Then she dragged Annie over to the computer, where Mick had pulled up three love emails.

The first questions were easy to answer. Annie advised both female readers to find new boyfriends, preferably ones with brains. But the third email had her stumped:

> Dear Professor Love,
>
> I love your column. (There's that word again — love.) But please don't give me a funny answer. As much as I love reading them, it's not what I need. I think I love John, but I'm not sure. How do I know for sure? I mean, what is love? What does it mean? Tell me what it looks like so I can know if I have it, and if John has it.
>
> — Sincerely, Simple

Annie sat back and stared at the screen.

"Annie, what's wrong?" Mick asked.

Before Annie could answer, Gracie, Queen of Observation, spoke up. "Well, look at this. It's finally happened. Unless I miss my guess, our own Professor Love is stumped."

10

"I'm not saying I'm stumped, exactly," Annie protested weakly, defending her reputation as Professor Love.

She could think of half a dozen funny comebacks for "Sincerely Simple." But that's not what the girl wanted ... or needed. Annie had to admit she'd been pretty free with the word *love*. She'd told her friends she was in love with Sean. What had she meant when she said it?

"Are you sure you've got this covered?" Gracie challenged. "Because those aren't the vibes I'm picking up on."

"Okay. You're right!" Annie cried. "I need help."

She waited until they gathered around her at the computer and could read the email for themselves. "So, what do I say? How do *I* know if she loves John or not?" She tried to think how she'd describe what she felt for Sean. "How about this? 'You love him if you think about him all the time and would rather be with him than with anybody'?"

"Sounds lame to me," Jazz said.

Annie had to agree.

"Try flipping the question around," Jazz suggested. "How would this girl know if John loves *her*?"

Again, Annie thought about Sean. She was pretty sure he
felt for her what she felt for him. But how *did* she know? The
way he smiled at her. He always looked happy to see her.
He'd asked *her* to homecoming. Yet none of that really added
up to a definition of *love*.

"Come on, Professor," Storm coaxed. "I wouldn't mind
hearing the answer to this one myself. Define *love* for us."

Annie turned back to the screen, as if the computer
had the answer.

"Annie," Mick said softly, "why don't you use First
Corinthians 13?"

"The 'Love Chapter,'" Annie said. Why hadn't she even
once thought to look there when she was thinking about Sean
or trying to be Professor Love?

"I give," Storm said. "What's First Whatever Thirteen?"

Mick ran over to her backpack and came back with a
purple Bible.

"Are you sure we want to go there with the blog?" Jazz
asked, like she was sure she didn't.

"Read it, Mick," Gracie said.

Mick cleared her throat and read: "'Love is patient, love is
kind. It does not envy, it does not boast, it is not proud. It is
not rude, it is not self-seeking, it is not easily angered, it keeps
no record of wrongs.'"

"Not bad," Gracie interrupted.

"Not easy," Jazz muttered.

"That's the catch," Mick explained. "It's impossible ...
unless it comes from God. There's more, too. Like that love
rejoices with truth and always protects and trusts and hopes
and never fails."

Annie's cell rang. She saw right away it was Sean. "Sean, let me call you back." She couldn't have said why she didn't want to talk to him right now.

"Don't hang up," Sean coaxed. "You want to drive around?"

"Not really, Sean." Her gaze landed on her dress, flung over the chair. "I could use a lift, though. I've got my homecoming dress here, at Gracie's cottage. I need to get it home."

"I'll be right over then."

Mick typed in the Love Chapter verses to answer the last email. Then Jazz, Storm, and Gracie headed over to the field with Mick. Annie planned to have Sean drop her off there after she left her dress at home.

She watched out the window for Sean. When she couldn't do that another minute, she got out her dress and held it up in front of the mirror

Where was he? Annie checked out the window again. It was almost dark. Mick was probably looking for her. She didn't want to let the Munch down, not again. She thought about calling Sean on his cell. But calling a guy to ask why he was late was a no-no. *Annie's Rule.*

Finally, she heard a horn beep outside. She hung up her dress and zipped the cover so Sean couldn't see it. The horn honked again. And again.

Annie raced out of the cottage, started down the walk, then remembered she had to lock up.

The horn honked again.

Sean wasn't alone. Stephen and Jon were scrunched into the back of the VW. They were both so big that it was like seeing a mass of guys.

Annie climbed into the front and had to fold her dress on her lap. "Hey, guys," she managed. "Sean, we better hurry. I promised Mick I'd go to her softball practice after we drop off the dress."

"Are you seriously going to watch a bunch of middle-school kids try to hit a ball?" Jon asked.

Sean turned to Annie. "Do we really have to do this, Annie?"

"Yep."

He sighed. "Okay. But we have to pick up our wedding tuxes first. The rental place will be closed if we don't." He turned onto Highway 42 and headed to the interstate, going east toward Cleveland.

An hour later, the boys were back in the car, their tuxes on their laps. And Annie was fuming.

"I still can't believe Coach is making us pay to rent these tuxes," Jon complained. "We're doing *him* the favor, ushering at his wedding."

"It's supposed to be an honor to be an usher, Jon," Annie said, glimpsing the guys in the rearview mirror. It was taking everything she had not to blow up at all of them.

"Some honor," Stephen griped. "A hundred bucks to rent? Couldn't we have bought a tux for that?"

"Keep it for the dance," Sean suggested.

Annie kept quiet while the guys exchanged stories and one-liners, mostly about sports or other players. She thought about homecoming and tried to get psyched about Sean in his tux and her in her new dress. But all she could imagine was her mom ... dancing with Hamlet.

Annie thought she should confide in Sean about Mom and Hamlet. But she wasn't sure how Sean would react.

Halfway back, they got stuck in traffic. Annie tried not to think about Mick looking for her and wondering what had happened to her. When they finally got back to town, Annie made Sean cruise by the middle-school field, even though she knew nobody would be there. She was right. The field was deserted.

She asked Sean to drop her off at home, and he didn't argue.

Sunday morning, Annie and her mom ate breakfast together, both pretending everything was fine. Neither of them brought up homecoming, but it loomed between them like an invisible wall.

Before the service started, Annie found Mick and Gracie and apologized for missing Mick's practice. "I really wanted to be there, Munch."

"That's okay," Mick said. "You didn't miss much. I don't know if I'll ever be able to pitch my best to those guys."

"I told her she should bean that little Kyle twerp," Gracie muttered.

"Gracie!" Mick chided.

"He gives Mick such a hard time," Gracie explained.

Mick sighed. "I can't pitch to him. He ... he just makes me so nervous. If he's up to bat against me on Saturday at final tryouts, I'll get cut for sure."

"You can't let him get to you, Mick!" Annie protested.

Mick tried to smile, but Annie could tell she was faking.

The music started, and Annie took her seat. But for the whole service, she couldn't stop stealing glances at Mick and feeling guilty for letting her down.

After church, Annie spent the rest of the day in her room, trying to catch up on homework. She could hear her mom in the kitchen, cooking up meals ahead of time so they'd have quick dinners in the freezer. It felt like they were strangers in the same house.

By dinner, she couldn't take it any longer. Her mother was her mother. And even if she was making this terrible mistake and going to homecoming with Hamlet, Annie loved her mom.

She crawled off her bed, where she'd been trying to study for the big *Romeo and Juliet* test, and started down the hall. Annie knew it was the right thing to do to make up with Mom. It's what her father would have wanted, if he were alive. She'd even apologize for losing her temper and saying things she didn't mean. Then she'd show Mom the dress she'd bought for homecoming, and things could be like they'd always been between them.

She was almost to the kitchen when she heard voices.

Something in her mind dismissed the sound as radio or TV noise. "Mom, I wanted — "

Annie stopped, the words freeze-dried to her tongue. Sitting at the kitchen table was Hamlet.

"Annie?" Her mom's smile twitched. "Look who dropped by to … to talk about homecoming."

Annie knew she was staring, but she couldn't stop. Hamlet in sweats and a baggy Ohio State sweatshirt barely looked like Hamlet.

"Hi, Annie. We've missed you at homecoming committee. You're not the only one backing out on us." He turned to Mom. "If it weren't for Jasmine Fletcher, we'd all be dancing under plain chicken wire."

Mom laughed as if that were the funniest thing anybody had ever said.

"We were just talking about the wedding," Mom tried.

"I thought you were just talking about homecoming," Annie snapped.

"Well, we were," Mom insisted. "Then Holden ... Mr. Hamilton ... brought up Coach Ramsey's football wedding." They both laughed, like they had some secret joke going.

Annie bit her tongue so she wouldn't say what she was thinking. A steely silence shrouded the room.

Hamlet sat up straighter. "Look. I'm really sorry if I've done anything to upset your family, Annie. Your mother and I are just friends. She mentioned she was going to the wedding, and I said I could stop by for her. No big deal. You're welcome to come too."

"Thanks, but no thanks," Annie said firmly.

"Anyway," he continued, "the last thing I'd want to do is make trouble for you or your mom. I don't want you to feel funny about this."

"Well," Annie said, "don't worry about that one. The last thing I feel about 'this,' is funny." Annie ran from the room so they couldn't see her cry.

11

Homecoming week was usually Annie's favorite week of school. But this homecoming seemed to drain all the pep out of her, instead of psyching her up. She'd thought up most of the spirit week activities herself. Monday was "Tacky Day," when students and teachers could get away with wearing just about anything. Tuesday was "Hawaiian Victory Day." The halls filled with Hawaiian tourist shirts, dark glasses, and even some grass skirts. Storm took advantage and came as the Mayan princess she claimed to be. On Wednesday, it was poodle skirts and bobby sox. Thursday, anything retro worked. And it all came together on Friday, when the whole school decked out in green and gold, except for Gracie, who proudly wore black and black.

Gracie's blog about homecoming was vintage Gracie. Jazz claimed it was her best ever:

• •

THAT'S WHAT YOU THINK!
by Jane
SEPTEMBER 19
SUBJECT: HOMECOMING

Why do they call it "homecoming"?

I've asked around. And the answer appears to be that old high school graduates "come home." (So why not "Comehoming"?) But what about the rest of us, the ones still in school, forced to go through homecoming rituals and pretend we're as excited as the cheerleaders?

At Typical High, we have a homecoming week, as if it's not enough torture to have a homecoming weekend. I call it "What Not to Wear Week." We're told how to dress each day. So everyone shows up, say, in '50s-style clothes, looking exactly alike, and telling themselves how nonconformist they all are. Think Halloween, without the candy.

And who invented school colors? I've yet to see a pair of school colors I'd allow in my closet.

While we're on the subject, what exactly is "pep"? First, it's the same backward as forward, which always makes me suspicious (I don't know about you). I can't say for sure about the mysterious origins of the word pep, but it sounds dangerously close to "pepper." As with that particular spice, a little goes a very long way. So do we really need more of it? Do we need all these rallies on behalf of pep? I think not.

Let me say it again: A little pep goes a long way.

Let's all be thankful that homecoming comes but once a year.

Annie laughed when she read the part about pep, remembering that Gracie had first blogged about Annie's pep, calling her "Bouncy Perky Girl." What had started out as an all-out fight had ended up a five-way blog friendship.

Annie was especially grateful for her blogging buddies during homecoming week. When she dropped out of the homecoming committee altogether, Jazz and Storm covered for her. Storm was amazing at pulling together costumes. Not only did she get her homecoming outfit from Goodwill, but she outfitted Annie and Jazz for "What Not to Wear Week."

The only one who didn't come through for Annie was Sean. There was still nobody Annie would rather go to homecoming with, of course. But he could be like two different people. Around the guys, he acted like Annie was a lawn ornament, something to decorate his world but not interfere with it.

Friday night, Annie cheered her heart out at the homecoming game, but it didn't help. Big Lake lost, 28 to 6. Sean had made plans with the guys to hang with Coach Ramsey after the game. But on Saturday, Sean was driving Annie to the wedding, and they were planning to spend the whole day together before going to the dance.

When Annie rolled out of bed Saturday morning, Mom was waiting for her. "Annie, I don't like this tension between us. I loved your father with everything I had. I still love him. I still miss him. But honey, chaperoning homecoming with Holden, or going to the wedding with him, doesn't mean I love your dad less. Or you."

Annie knew Mom was right. Her mom's love had always been the one thing Annie could count on, the thing she never doubted.

"I love you, Annie."

"I know," Annie whispered. "I love you too." She squeezed her eyes shut to keep back the tears. They came anyway, and she let them.

She felt her mom's arms wrap around her. They stood like that for a while, holding each other. When Mom finally let go, she said, "Hey. Don't you think it's about time I saw that homecoming dress of yours?"

Annie showed her the dress and couldn't have hoped for a better reaction.

"You need backless shoes, black — mine!" Mom ran to her bedroom and came back with the exact pair Annie would have chosen. "I don't think they'll hurt your feet. They're a little big on me. Plus, there's no back strap."

Annie tried them on. Her feet were nearly a size larger than her mom's, but the shoes worked. "They're perfect," she said. "But what will you wear?"

Mom shrugged. "Maybe tennis shoes? In case I have to make a getaway? I've never chaperoned high school kids before." She laughed, then fingered her hair. "I'm more worried about this hair."

"You always look great," Annie assured her.

Mom glanced at her sideways. "And you know good and well you'd never be caught dead with hair like this."

They both got ready for the wedding. Annie knew Sean and the other ushers were supposed to get to the field early, but Hamlet was the first to show up at the Lind house. Unlike Annie's date, her English teacher rang the doorbell and waited patiently.

Annie had to wait twenty minutes after Hamlet and Mom left before she heard Sean's honk. She dashed to the VW, disappointed to see Stephen and Jon in the backseat.

"I see the gang's all here," she said, not trying to hide the sarcasm.

"Yeah," Sean said. He so did not get it.

"Maybe Annie will know," Jon said from the back.

She turned around. "Know what?"

"What's this wedding stuff going to do to our football field?" Stephen asked. "High heels and chairs — that's going to mess up the field."

"I told you," Sean explained, taking off too fast, "we put a tarp down."

"That's a lot of trouble," Jon complained.

Annie wheeled on the backseat boys. "It's a wedding, boys. It's supposed to be a lot of trouble."

"I thought trouble came *after* the wedding," Sean joked.

The backseat boys laughed.

Annie felt anger bubbling in her chest, and she wasn't even sure why. "Look, guys. This is an important day for Coach. He's waited a long time to find the right woman."

"No kidding," Jon agreed. "Fran too. She's pretty old to be getting married, if you ask me."

Annie started to defend Coach's bride, but Sean beat her to it.

"Come on, guys. Fran was taking her time. It's a big decision choosing the man your children will spend every other weekend with for the rest of their lives."

Stephen and Jon laughed so hard Annie didn't even try for a comeback. Why couldn't Sean have come alone? She was beginning to wonder if he went anywhere without his buddies. She, on the other hand, had dropped her friends whenever Sean had other plans for her.

She wished she hadn't done that. She'd really never thought of it as dropping them. But all he had to do was walk by, and she'd left her friends to follow him.

Annie was surprised how many people were already on the football field when they got there. The tarp covered the field to the 40-yard line. Folding chairs made straight rows in two sections. Flowers wound around the goalposts, turning them into a wedding arch. Apparently, the ceremony would take place in the end zone.

"It's pretty, don't you think?" Annie asked, holding Sean's arm as they crossed the 20-yard line.

Sean tried, and failed, to muffle a laugh. "I still think it's crazy. I better find out what I'm supposed to do in this circus."

Not much, Annie thought, *since you're too late to seat most of the wedding guests.*

She found Storm and Gracie on the 15-yard line and climbed into the one empty chair in the middle of the row, next to Gracie.

From the sidelines came a shout, "Let's go!" Everyone turned around. Annie felt like slinking in her chair when she saw Sean leading the ushers in a team huddle.

"And they call *us* the weaker sex?" Gracie commented.

Annie glanced around. Most of the guests were teachers and students. "Have you seen Mom and Hamlet yet?" she whispered to Gracie.

"Yeah. You okay with it? They're up there." Gracie pointed to about the 2-yard line, where Mom and Hamlet were sitting. And next to them sat Granny and Gramps Lind.

"I can't believe it!" Annie exclaimed. "They're all sitting together. What happened?" Granny was smiling, and Gramps was pointing at the goalposts and saying something to Hamlet.

Annie got up and worked her way out of the row. "I've got to see this."

Gramps was on the aisle, so Annie knelt beside his chair and tapped his shoulder.

"Annie!" he cried. "You look gorgeous, sweetie."

"Thanks, Gramps." She nodded toward Hamlet and Mom. "How did you guys ...? I mean, when did you — ?"

"When did we stop being stupid, do you mean?" He grinned at her, and something about his smile looked exactly like her favorite photo of her dad, the one she kept on her dresser.

"I wouldn't have worded it that way," she said, grinning at Granny.

Granny leaned over and said, "Annie, we were a couple of knuckleheads. It took the Lord a little time, but he brought us around. He always does."

The marching band started up from the opposite end zone. Granny's words echoed in Annie's ears as she rushed back to her seat: *He brought us around. He always does.* Annie slipped into her row of seats. "Gracie, when are Mick's tryouts?"

"Right after the wedding. I'm jetting over there ASAP."

"Me too," Storm said.

Sean and Stephen took the two empty chairs behind Annie and Storm. "Come on back, Annie!" Sean begged. "You can sit on my lap."

"I'll pass, thanks," Annie answered, wishing he would be quiet.

The band marched down the field. It was weird hearing the Wedding March as a real march. Six bridesmaids, dressed in green and gold, of course, walked the long white makeshift aisle through the crowd and into the end zone.

When the bride appeared, everyone stood up. It was a long wait as Fran made her way one hundred yards to the goalposts.

Sean and Stephen never stopped whispering asides: "Run, Fran!" "Backfield in motion!" "Go out for a pass!" "First and 40!" "Drop back and punt!"

As the bride passed Annie's row, Annie studied Fran's face. She'd never make the cover of *Brides* magazine. Her features looked like someone had tossed them onto her face, meaning to come back for them later. She was tall and skinny, with red hair and a toothy grin. But the pure happiness in her eyes made her look beautiful.

As Coach Ramsey watched his bride, he smiled, as if he were the proudest man on earth. Nobody could doubt that this bride and groom were in love.

Love. Even thinking the word threw Annie into confusion. Did she have any idea what love meant?

12

Sean leaned up and whispered in Annie's ear, "How much longer till it's over?"

Annie turned and stared at him. Sean was so handsome. She still felt like melting when he smiled at her. But that wasn't love.

"Dearly beloved — " The speakers squealed, and the crowd groaned, just like they did at games. "We are gathered here in the sight of God ..."

Annie closed her eyes and sank into the knowledge that she was in the sight of God. *I'm sorry I don't think about you more,* she began. *But I'm grateful that you go with me everywhere, even to this football wedding. I really do want you in every part of my life.*

She listened to every word as the pastor told Fran and Coach that their love for each other should reflect Christ's love for them. Then Fran's sister, who looked just like Fran, tall, thin, with bright red hair, took the microphone and read "the Love Chapter" from the Bible.

" 'Love is patient, love is kind. It does not envy, it does not boast, it is not proud ...' "

It was the same passage Mick had come up with to define *love*. But this time the words felt like pinpricks.

" 'It is not rude, it is not self-seeking, it is not easily angered, it keeps no record of wrongs. Love does not delight in evil but rejoices with the truth. It always protects, always trusts, always hopes, always perseveres. Love never fails.' "

Sean let out a laugh behind her. Annie couldn't help measuring him against this definition of *love*. Love isn't rude? Wasn't it rude to make fun of the most important day in Fran's and Coach's lives? Wasn't it rude to be late picking her up? Love isn't self-seeking? What else did Sean do but look out for himself? How could she have blown off her friends for someone so rude and insensitive and full of himself?

Annie felt her stomach knot with anger.

Love is not easily angered.

And what about *her*?

Annie replayed the past two weeks. She'd been angry at Mom, angry with Sean. *Love is patient. Love is kind. It does not envy ... It is not self-seeking ...* She'd been so intent on getting Sean to take her to homecoming, she hadn't had time to be kind to anybody else. She'd felt that stupid envy over Storm and Cody. She hadn't even tried to make things better between her mom and grandparents. She'd been too caught up in her own life. She hadn't even tried to help Mick.

I'm so sorry! She said it to herself first. Then she said it to God. She let her mind run through the definition of *love* again. But this time, she thought about God, the way God loved her, in spite of how stupid and selfish she'd been. God was patient and kind with her. He wouldn't give up on her.

Then she thought of Mick. The Munch came as close to this definition of *love* as anybody Annie knew. Talk about patient, and kind, and looking out for everybody else ...

The drums rolled, and the band played, and Annie realized the wedding was over.

"I'm out of here," Gracie said, standing up.

Storm stood up too. "See you tonight, Annie. We gotta jet. Mick might be on the mound right now."

Annie ached to go with them, but she knew Sean wouldn't want to.

"Man, I thought it'd never be over!" Sean exclaimed. He pushed chairs aside to get to Annie. "Come on! At least we can get something to eat at the reception."

"Sean, I have to go to Mick's tryouts."

"Now?"

"You can do the reception without me, and we can meet up later. Okay?" She eased out of the row of chairs.

"No, it's not okay," Sean whined. He turned to Stephen. "What time are we leaving, man?"

"Right after the reception, dude," Stephen answered.

Annie didn't get it. "The dance isn't until eight."

Sean lowered his voice. "Yeah, but Bridget's party's probably started already."

"Bridget's party?" It was the first Annie had heard about *this* plan.

"You'll have a blast!" Stephen promised. "Right, Sean?"

Annie should have seen this coming. "I won't go to that party."

The field was emptying. Annie saw Gracie and Storm weaving through the crowd, cutting over toward the middle school.

Sean screwed up his face like a little boy. "Don't be like that, Annie. I want to go to Bridget's with everybody."

Annie studied his perfect face and eyes. He was so cute. But that was all. And it wasn't enough. "Then go," she said quietly.

"Huh?" Sean frowned, then glanced at Stephen and back to her. "I'm not kidding, Annie. I can get another date to homecoming."

"Good idea," she said calmly. She turned and started running toward the middle school.

"Annie!" Sean called after her.

She didn't turn around as she raised a hand and waved. "Have fun, Sean!"

Annie ran all the way to the middle school and found Gracie and Storm sitting with Jazz in the bleachers. "Where's Mick?" she shouted, climbing three rows to get to them.

"Annie!" Storm exclaimed. "What are you doing here? Where's Sean?"

"Last seen on the 15-yard line, looking for a date to homecoming," she answered.

"Way to go, Annie!" Gracie shouted. "The things I could tell you about that guy's body language . . ."

"Look!" Jazz interrupted. "Mick's pitching to that kid again, the one who's been giving her so much trouble."

"Kyle," Gracie muttered.

Mick stood on the mound, looking so little that Annie wanted to run out and hug her. "Go, Mick!" she cried.

"I don't think she heard you," Gracie said. "I can't believe she got this guy as first batter!"

"Play ball!" Coach Yardley hollered.

Mick nodded.

Kyle shouted something out to Mick from the batter's box. Mick looked like she was sick. She wound up and pitched. Even Annie could tell it was high and wide.

"Man, he's doing it again!" Jazz said. "That kid really gets to her."

Annie leaped off the bleachers and charged onto the field. She heard Gracie calling her to come back, but she didn't slow down until she was on the mound.

"Annie? You can't be here," Mick said.

Coach Yardley jogged onto the field, shouting, "Annie Lind, what do you think you're doing?"

"Calling a time-out," Annie answered. "Will you please excuse us for a minute?"

He started to protest, then threw his hands into the air. "One minute. That's it!"

"Annie," Mick started, "thanks for coming. But you can't be out here."

"Listen to me, Mick." She glanced at the batter, then back to Mick. "I'm going to ask you to do something, and you're going to have to trust me. I know you don't have any reason to trust me, not after the way I've let you down lately."

"Of course I trust you, Annie."

"I'm starting to understand some things about love, thanks to you, Mick."

"Thanks to *me*?" Mick glanced nervously at her coach.

"Love's a powerful thing, Mick. Here's what I want you to do. Before you pitch to Kyle, I want you to tell him you love him."

"Annie! I can't do that!"

"Please, Mick. You and I will know you love him because Mick the Munch loves everybody, right? But Kyle is going to have to think about that one."

Mick started to shake her head.

"Please, Mick. Trust me. Will you do it?"

"Minute's up!" Coach yelled. "Play ball or sit down!"

"I love you, Mick," Annie whispered. "And you already know God loves you, even if you never get a good pitch to this guy. So you go, girl!"

Annie ran back and took her seat.

From the bleachers, all she could see were Mick's lips moving. Then Kyle's mouth dropped open. The poor guy looked like he didn't know what hit him. And for the next three pitches, he didn't. Three strikes, and he was out.

Mick struck out the next two batters and caught a line drive from the third. Then Coach had her pitch to him. He hit her a couple of times, but her curve was awesome.

When she was done, Mick ran over to the bleachers. "I did it! Coach said I'm on the team!"

"He better say that," Annie said, "unless he wants to deal with us, right?"

Gracie and Storm and Jazz seconded that.

They fell into step and, without discussing it, headed toward the cottage together.

"I thought you had plans with Sean all day," Mick said.

"So did I," Annie commented. "Turns out we were all wrong about that. Guess who's not going to homecoming."

"Truly a moment in Typical High history!" Gracie walked backward so she could face Annie. "Annie Lind? Dateless for homecoming? Bouncy Perky Girl? Professor Love? What's the world coming to?"

"No fair," Storm complained. "So I'm the only blogger going?"

"You really broke your date with Sean?" Jazz asked.

"Yup. So, what do you say to a movie night at the cottage? Anything but a romance flick."

Annie made plans to meet Gracie, Mick, and Jazz at the cottage and bring the popcorn. But first, she ran home to check on Mom. She found her wrestling with her hair in front of the bathroom mirror.

"Looks like you could use a hand," Annie observed.

"You're not kidding! But don't you have to get yourself ready?"

Annie French-braided Mom's hair as she brought her up to date on the Sean disaster.

"I'm so sorry, honey," Mom said after Annie had given her the details. "Are you sure you're okay staying home tonight? You could always come to the dance with Holden and me."

They both laughed, and it felt good. "Aside from the fact that I'd rather stick hot needles under my fingernails, as Storm would say, I have other plans."

When Hamlet rang the doorbell, fifteen minutes early, Annie and Marbles opened the door. Annie even managed to carry on a pretty normal conversation with him until her mother came out.

"Don't stay out too late," Annie cautioned, using her mother's favorite line. She felt a little twinge as she watched them walk to the car together. But Holden Hamilton looked as uncomfortable in his homecoming suit as Gracie would have in Annie's homecoming dress. And somehow that made her feel better.

The rest of the night, Annie watched a movie marathon with Gracie, Mick, and Jazz at the cottage. It felt weird knowing that the homecoming dance was going on without her, that Sean probably had another date and was dancing with her right now.

But her friends kept her laughing and eating. And she had to admit she was having fun ... without a guy.

During the third movie, Annie slipped away. She'd promised Gracie a homecoming column, and that's what she was going to write.

• •

THAT'S WHAT YOU THINK!

SEPTEMBER 20
SUBJECT: HOMECOMING

It's homecoming night. And while Typical High school students are out dancing in the tissue-stuffed gym, your very own Professor Love sits here dateless. Yes, you heard it here first. No date to homecoming.

I had a date, but now I don't. Why? you ask. Because I figured out that I, Professor Love, seem to suffer from the Dorothy Syndrome. Like our little female friend from Oz, I seem to attract men who need a heart, a brain, or a bit of courage.

But that's not my main problem.

In the past twenty-four hours, I've discovered some things about myself and about love. I was planning on writing a big column about the homecoming dance. But since I'm not there, you'll have to settle for my personal revelations.

I've discovered that I don't know as much about love as I thought I did. I thought I was in love because I went weak in the knees whenever I saw this guy, because I couldn't stop thinking about him. That may be a little part of what love is. But love's a lot more. Check out that definition my friend found for love in the last blog. You won't find anything "weak in the knees" about that kind of love. It's strong, patient, and kind. And it comes from God, not from psyching ourselves up over somebody we barely know.

I'm missing the homecoming dance. And guess what — the world hasn't fallen apart. (Not that I don't plan to be at homecoming next year, mind you!) I'm having fun with some friends who are also missing homecoming. And hanging out with friends isn't so bad. In fact, I think friendship may even be a kind of love.

What I'm discovering is that there are shades of love, and romance is just one of those shades. Love's a lot more than I thought it was. Your Professor Love has a lot to learn about love.

So stay tuned. There's much more to come.

Internet Safety

by Michaela

People aren't always what they seem at first, like wolves in sheep's clothing. Chat rooms, blogs, and other places online can be fun ways to meet all kinds of people with all kinds of interests. But be aware and cautious. Here are some tips to help keep you safe while surfing the web, keeping a blog, chatting online, and writing emails.

• Never give out personal information such as your address, phone number, parents' work addresses or phone numbers, or the name and address of your school without your parents' or guardian's permission. It's okay to talk about your likes and dislikes, but keep private information just that—private.

• Before you agree to meet someone in person, first check with your parents or guardian to make sure it's okay. A safe way to meet for the first time is to bring a parent or guardian with you.

• You might be tempted to send a picture of yourself to new friends you've met online. Just in case your acquaintance is not who you think they are, check with your parent or guardian before you hit send.

• If you feel uncomfortable by angry, threatening, or other types of emails or posts addressed to you, tell your parent or guardian immediately.

• Before you promise to call a new friend on the telephone, talk to your parent or guardian first.

• Remember that just because you might read about something or someone online doesn't mean the information is true. Sometimes people say cruel or untruthful things just to be mean.

• If someone writes creepy posts, report him or her to the blog or website owner.

Following these tips will help keep you safe while you hang out online. If you're careful, you can learn a lot and meet tons of new people.

Subject: Michaela Jenkins

Age: 13 on May 19, 7th grade at Big Lake Middle School
Hair/Eyes: Dark brown hair/Brown eyes
Height: 5'

"Mick the Munch" is content and rooted in her relationship with Christ. She lives with her step-sis, Grace Doe, in the blended family of Gracie's dad and Mick's mom. She's a tomboy, an avid Cleveland Indians fan, and the only girl on her school's baseball team. A computer whiz, Mick keeps *That's What You Think!* up and running. She also helps out at Sam's Sammich Shop and manages to show her friends what deep faith looks like.

Subject: Grace Doe

Age: 15 on August 19, sophomore
Hair/Eyes: Blonde hair/Hazel eyes
Height: 5', 5"

Grace doesn't think she is cute at all. The word "average" was meant for her. She dresses in neutral colors and camouflage to blend in. Grace does not wear makeup. She prefers to observe life rather than participate in it. A bagger at a grocery store, only her close friends and family can get away with calling her "Gracie." She is part of a blended family and lives with Dad and step-mom, two step-siblings, and two half brothers. Her mother's job frequently keeps her out of town.

Subject: Annie Lind

Age: 16 on October 1, sophomore
Hair/Eyes: Auburn hair/Blue eyes
Height: 5', 10"

Annie desperately wants guys to admire and like her. She is boy-crazy and thinks she always has to be in love. She considers herself to be an expert in matters of the heart. Annie takes being popular for granted because she has always been well-liked. She loves and admires her mom. Her dad was killed in a plane crash when Annie was two months old. Annie helps out at Sam's Sammich Shop, her mom's restaurant. She can be self-centered, though without being selfish.

Subject: Jasmine Fletcher

Age: 15 on July 13, freshman
Hair/Eyes: Black hair/Brown eyes
Height: 5', 6"

Jasmine is an artist who feels that no one, especially her art teacher and parents, understands her art. She is African American, and has great fashion sense, without being trendy. Her parents are quite well-to-do, and they won't let Jasmine get a job. She has a younger brother and a sister who has Down syndrome. She also had a brother who was killed in a drive-by shooting in the old neighborhood when Jazz was one.

Subject: Storm Novello

Age: 14 on September 1, freshman
Hair/Eyes: Brown hair/Dark brown eyes
Height: 5', 2"

Storm doesn't realize how pretty she is. She wishes she had blonde hair. She is Mayan/Mestisa, and claims to be a Mayan princess. Storm always needs to be the center of attention and doesn't let on how smart she is. She dresses in bright, flouncy clothing, and wears too much makeup. Storm is a completely different person around her parents. She changes into her clothes and puts her makeup on after leaving for school. Her parents are very loving, though they have little money.

Here's a sneak preview of the next book in the Faithgirlz! Blog On! series, now available!

1

Jazz Fletcher stormed outside, slamming the door behind her. But the giant cedar door to the Fletcher mansion didn't slam. It *swooshed* shut.

Great, Jazz thought, as she stared up at the gray, cloudless sky. *It's not enough that everyone in my house is against me. The house itself hates me.*

She shook her head to try to get rid of her mother's last words — Jazz's mother always got the last word: "Jazz, you'll have time to play with your paints and things in the summer. The school year is for *real* classes."

Jazz and her parents had argued about her art so often, Jazz could have performed both sides of the argument word for word. But it didn't matter. She was going to be an artist, no matter what they thought.

Jazz took off for Gracie's cottage, walking so fast that the crisp October air tickled her nostrils. Grace Doe had started a website, *That's What You Think!*, where she'd blogged her observations about people. Now a team of girls ran the site, and Jazz's job was, of course, art design — graphics and an occasional cartoon. Jazz figured she'd be late to their weekly meeting, thanks to her mother.

Jazz was almost to the cottage when she noticed a waft of smoke, filtered and flavored, through someone's chimney. She sniffed the air and thought she could even smell the color of the red orange maple leaves, softer than the yellow ginkgos still clinging to branches. She'd have given anything to have her canvas and paints right now. She'd capture it all, including the hint of gasoline from a mower. She would take the unseen smells and turn them into a masterpiece.

A horn honked.

Jazz realized she was standing in the middle of the road. It wasn't a busy street. But the red Honda obviously didn't have time for teenaged artists. She took in one last breath and trotted to the sidewalk.

What if the picture she'd had in her head seconds ago, the painting of autumn smells, could have been her masterpiece? The one thing that would make everybody, especially her art-hating parents, sit up and take notice? Already the vision faded, the reds becoming less red, the umber washing to pale yellow.

She walked the rest of the way to Gracie's cottage. Jazz was pretty sure a couple of her friends would have given her grief for throwing in with Gracie's group, if they'd known about it. But *That's What You Think!* was anonymous. Big Lake High was "Typical High," and Gracie made up funny names for everybody she blogged about. And anyway, being part of the blog was one of the few good things going on in Jazz's life right now, not that she'd ever say it out loud.

Jazz knocked on the cottage door, then walked on in. "Anybody home?" She inhaled the lilac and musty smell of the cottage. The place belonged to Gracie's mom, who was almost always traveling in Europe. Gracie had started trying to get the group together Saturday mornings, and this was their base of operation.

"You're late," Gracie mumbled, taking Jazz's jacket when she shrugged out of it.

"Guilty," Jazz replied.

Gracie was pretty straight-up. What you saw was what you got.

Jazz appreciated that. She could imagine doing an abstract portrait of Grace Doe. Instead of painting Gracie's short, straight, blonde hair and big, hazel eyes in a glorified snapshot, the way their art teacher encouraged them to paint, Jazz would center the abstract on a tiny scar above Gracie's right eyebrow. The scar was so thin and short that Jazz knew nobody ever noticed it, except her. But to Jazz, the scar said everything. It symbolized a pain inside of Gracie, something caused by her parents' divorce, when her mom had left Gracie with her dad. That scar seemed to have healed over too, more or less. Jazz had asked Gracie about the scar once, and it was nothing more than a cut from an old bicycle accident. Not to Jazz.

Mick, Gracie's little stepsis and the blog's technical guru, was already clicking away at the computer keys. "Hey, Jazz!" she called.

"Hey yourself, Munch." Jazz handed Mick the cartoon she'd drawn earlier in the week and leaned on the back of Mick's chair. As always, Mick took the drawing without looking or showing it to anybody, flipped it over, and placed it in the scanner. In seconds, she had the colorized sketch uploaded. Jazz and Gracie crowded at the edges of the screen.

"That rocks!" Mick exclaimed, adjusting the scanned image.

"Excellent," Gracie agreed.

Jazz brushed off the praise, but she clung to it on the inside. It felt good to have somebody appreciate her work for a change. She changed the subject before Gracie had a chance to "read" her. The girl was an expert in observing gestures and picking up on signs of emotion, little things nobody else would notice. "So why aren't Storm and Annie here?"

"I don't know about Storm. Annie had cheerleading or something," Mick explained. "But she dropped off her 'Professor Love' column."

"Let's see it." Jazz reached over and jiggled the mouse to wake the screen from sleep mode.

Gracie threw herself in front of the computer, blocking the screen. "Okay. Jazz, promise you won't get mad. Storm saw my blog, and she's okay with it."

"Gracie! You wrote about us again?" Jazz accused.

"True," Gracie admitted. "But Storm is still 'New Girl.' And I changed your name to 'Monet.'"

Jazz nudged Gracie away from the screen and started with her blog. "Should have changed my name to 'Van Gogh.' He never sold anything while he was alive either."

• • • • • • • • • • • • • • • • • • • •

THAT'S WHAT YOU THINK!
by Jane
OCTOBER 4
SUBJECT: A CONVERSATION WITH BODIES

So last week in art, New Girl got paired with Pastel Princess when we had to paint each other. Princess is a freshman, like New Girl, but there end the similarities. Without uttering a word to each other, their unspoken conversation went like this:

Pastel Princess:	*Clasped hands. ["Cool!"]*
New Girl:	*Angled her upper body thirty degrees away from Princess. ["You've got to be kidding."]*
Princess:	*Squared herself to face New Girl. ["You start, okay? Will you, huh?"]*
New Girl:	*Rubbed forehead ["Oh, man! Why me?"], crossed legs ["Let's get this over with."], and then placed palms down on desk. ["Okay. This is how it's going to be. Got it?"]*
Princess:	*Pulled arms and elbows into body. ["Whatever you say."]*
New Girl:	*Lifted face and chin. ["You got that right."]*

The body language between Monet and Perfect Guy was much shorter, but every bit as enlightening:

Monet:	*Arms crossed, with elbows high and pointed out. ["This is too cruel, even for the art teacher. No way I'm painting this guy."]*
Perfect Guy:	*Inhaled, balloon-like, keeping his profile to Monet. ["I, of course, shall begin. Watch how I do it and be enlightened."]*

"So who's Perfect Guy?" Mick asked.

Jazz had no trouble with that one. "Paul Brown," she answered. Gracie had nailed Paul. "His mother has an office on Dad's floor at Spiels Corporation. My parents think Paul Brown is perfect. So does Paul, for that matter. So do Paul's parents."

The second she said it, something twisted in her chest. Paul's parents did think their son was perfect. They came to every open house and fussed over each sketch or painting or sculpture Paul had on display.

Jazz walked off to the kitchen for a glass of water. She didn't want Gracie to see her, to *read* her, to read her thoughts by her gestures or expression. Not right now. Because what Jazz was thinking was what it must feel like to be Paul, to have your parents love everything you do in art. To have your parents think you were perfect.

It was something Jazz knew she would never have.

faiThGirLz!

2 corinthians 4:18

Inner Beauty, Outward Faith

Grace Notes

Softcover • ISBN 0-310-71093-6

Busted! An anonymous teenage blogger comes in from the cold... Gracie Doe, an astute observer of human nature, prefers blogging about her high school classmates to befriending them—and she likes being a loner just fine, thanks.

Just Jazz

Softcover • ISBN 0-310-71095-2

Jazz is working on a masterpiece: herself... Jasmine "Jazz" Fletcher is an artist down to her toes; she sees beauty and art where others see nothing. And her work on the website is drawing rave reviews. But if she doesn't come up with a commercially successful masterpiece pretty soon, her parents may make her drop what they consider an expensive hobby to focus on a real job.

Storm Rising

Softcover • ISBN 0-310-71096-0

Nobody knows the real Storm... not even Storm! The center of attention wherever she goes, Storm Novelo is impetuous, daring, loud—and a phony. Convinced that no one would like her inner brainiac, she hides her genius behind her public airhead.

Available now at your local bookstore!

zonderkidz

2 corinthians 4:18

Inner Beauty, Outward Faith

- -

With TNIV text and Faithgirlz™ sparkle, this Bible goes right to the heart of a girl's world and has a unique landscape format perfect for sharing.

The Faithgirlz™ TNIV Bible • Hardcover • 0-310-71002-2

The Faithgirlz™ TNIV Bible • Faux Fur • 0-310-71004-9

- -

Available now at your local bookstore!

zonderkidz

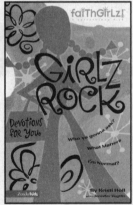

faiThGirLz!
2 corinthians 4:18

Inner Beauty, Outward Faith

Visit **faithgirlz.com**—
it's the place for girls ages 8-12!

We want to hear from you. Please send your comments about this
book to us in care of zreview@zondervan.com. Thank you.

ZONDERVAN.COM/
AUTHORTRACKER

zonderkidz

Grand Rapids, MI 49530
www.zonderkidz.com